"Is There Something Wrong With Your Food?"

"Not at all," Kate assured him. "There's just too much of it! And wanting to set an example for our baby, I've been trying to clean my plate."

"Our baby?" Until Trace murmured the question, Kate wasn't even aware of her odd choice of words.

"Our? Did I say our? I didn't mean to say our! Really, I meant *your* baby!" Kate knew she was chattering. The slow smile lifting the edges of Trace's lips didn't help much, either!

Casually leaning back in his chair, Trace slid an encompassing glance over Kate, then his daughter, Kathy, then Kate again. As if he'd come to an important decision, he nodded once.

"Kathy's beautiful," he said in that same low tone. "But you and I would make an equally beautiful child together...."

Dear Reader,

Welcome to Silhouette! Our goal is to give you hours of unbeatable reading pleasure, and we hope you'll enjoy each month's six new Silhouette Desires. These sensual, provocative love stories are both believable and compelling—sometimes they're poignant, sometimes humorous, but always enjoyable.

Indulge yourself. Experience all the passion and excitement of falling in love along with our heroine as she meets the irresistible man of her dreams and together they overcome all obstacles in the path to a happy ending.

If this is your first Desire, I hope it'll be the first of many. If you're already a Silhouette Desire reader, thanks for your support! Look for some of your favorite authors in the coming months: Stephanie James, Diana Palmer, Dixie Browning, Ann Major and Doreen Owens Malek, to name just a few.

Happy reading!

Isabel Swift
Senior Editor

JOAN
HOHL
A Much Needed
Holiday

Silhouette Desire

Published by Silhouette Books New York

America's Publisher of Contemporary Romance

SILHOUETTE BOOKS
300 E. 42nd St., New York, N.Y. 10017

Copyright © 1985 by Joan Hohl

Distributed by Pocket Books

ISBN: 0-373-05247-2

First Silhouette Books printing December 1985

10 9 8 7 6 5 4 3 2 1

America's Publisher of Contemporary Romance

Printed in the U.S.A.

JOAN HOHL,

a Gemini and an inveterate daydreamer, says she always has her head in the clouds. Though she reads eight or nine books a week, she only discovered romances ten years ago. "But as soon as I read one," she confesses, "I was hooked." Now, an extremely popular author, she is thrilled to be getting paid for exactly what she loves doing best. Joan Hohl also writes under the pseudonym Amii Lorin.

For Rita Clay Estrada,
for introducing me to San Antonio.
And for Kay Garteiser, Parris Afton Bonds,
Linda Lucas, Tate Mckenna, Gayle Link and Kathie Seidick
for their delightful company at dinner
along the San Antonio River walk.
Remember the Alamo!

One

Kate Warren never knew her parents. It wasn't as if Kate was an orphan, or that her parents had abandoned her when she was an infant. Kate merely never had the opportunity to get to know the two people who had made her birth possible. When it came right down to it, Kate's parents didn't know each other all that well either.

Since Kate had faced the fact that her parents were strangers, well over ten years ago around her thirteenth birthday, it no longer bothered her except during this time of the year—the season of goodwill, peace on earth, and strong family unity.

Slowly threading her way through the shoppers thronging to the mall on the Saturday after Thanksgiving Day, Kate smiled wistfully at a snowsuited toddler impeding her progress. The blond child's dark blue eyes were as wide as saucers as she gazed in wonder at the twinkling decorations on the Christmas tree that rose majestically into the air, thirty feet from its base in the center of the mall.

Sublimely unconcerned with the foot traffic of the giants scurrying around her, the child came to a dead stop, her tiny red lips forming a silent *oh* at the magical sight of animated animals and carollers dressed in Victorian garb at the foot of the mighty pine.

Enchanted by the toddler's rapt expression, Kate came to a halt only inches from her. Momentarily forgetting how pressed for time she was, Kate observed the child as she examined the man-made winter wonderland.

The child, little more than a baby really, was beautiful. Blond curls cascaded around her small shoulders and pooled into the tossed-back hood of her pink jacket. A tiny, not quite pointed, chin was raised as the child lifted her head to stare at the huge star at the very top of the tree. Her cheeks were downy soft and flushed with pleasure. Her blue eyes were bright from the reflection of the sparkling lights.

Sighing, Kate snapped herself out of the spell cast by the little girl and moved to walk around the child. At the same instant, the toddler blinked and gazed up trustingly. Before Kate could take a step, the expression on the tiny face changed from delight to terror, and her little lips parted to emit a wailing cry.

"Daddy!"

Her mouth soft, Kate glanced around, preparing to smile in understanding when her gaze encountered the child's anxious father or mother. Her smile turned into a frown when all she saw were curious looks from the people rushing by.

"I want my daddy!"

The now tearful sound of the child's high-pitched voice drew Kate's gaze back to her terrified little face. What the devil was she to do, Kate thought frantically, suddenly mindful of the time and the fact that she was already late for her lunch date. She simply couldn't walk away and leave this child standing all alone!

"It's all right, baby," Kate said soothingly, stooping to be on a level with the sobbing child. "Don't cry, honey."

Revealing incredibly long eyelashes, the child blinked again. "I want my daddy!" she cried loudly. "Where's my daddy?"

"I...I don't know, love." Uncomfortably aware of the stares she was receiving, Kate tentatively raised a hand to brush at the tears rolling down the small face. "I think he's lost."

Strangely, Kate's observation magically silenced the sobs. Frowning in a comically adult manner, the child stared at her.

"Daddy's lost?" she asked solemnly.

"I'm afraid so, baby. But don't worry, I'll help you find him," Kate promised reassuringly. "Come along, love." Standing, Kate held out her hand to the girl. "We'll go to the mall office." As the child slipped her small hand into hers, Kate smiled again, "I wouldn't be surprised if we found your daddy already there."

The child gazed up at her with innocent eyes. "Is that where lost daddies go?"

"Usually." Kate nodded. "And then, the lady or man working in the office will give a description of the lost daddy over the public address system."

"Oh." Wide blue eyes gazed at Kate uncomprehendingly.

Muffling a groan, Kate bit on her lip. How in the world did one go about explaining a public address system to a child three years old at the outside, she wondered, carefully guarding the little person as she wove in and out of the shoppers.

"Do you ever listen to the radio?" Kate asked hopefully.

"Yes." The little girl nodded eagerly.

"Well, the public address is something like the radio," Kate smiled. "You'll see when we get there, baby."

"Kathy."

Startled by the blandly delivered information, Kate stopped walking to stare at the child. "Your name's Kathy?" The girl nodded again. "That's a beautiful name," Kate complimented. "And my name is Kate." Beginning to move again, Kate paused when the child tugged on her hand.

"Is my daddy crying 'cause he's lost?" Kathy's lips trembled.

If he's not he ought to be, Kate thought, inwardly outraged at the very idea of a man being so careless with his daughter. Even in their disinterest her parents had never lost *her*! Hiding her feelings behind a smile, Kate shrugged helplessly.

"Does your daddy cry a lot?" she probed.

Kathy frowned in that oddly adult way. "No." She shook her head decisively. "Not ever."

Then perhaps he should, Kate declared mutely, picturing Kathy's father as a typical swaggering macho-man.

"Daddy don't like Christmas." Kathy offered the unsolicited information sadly. "Or Santa Claus," she added on a sniff.

"Daddy *doesn't* like Christmas," Kate corrected automatically.

"I know." Kathy sniffed again, louder this time. "He said he'd just as soon forget the whole blasted thing."

Kate's sense of outrage grew into consuming anger. Kathy had obviously quoted her father verbatim. What sort of man would say such a thing to a baby, she mused irritably, especially a beautiful, alert baby? Trying to keep her smile, Kate squeezed the small hand gently. *She* wasn't particularly wild about the holiday either, but she'd never dream of spoiling it for an innocent youngster.

"Why doesn't daddy like Christmas or Santa Claus, honey?" Kate inquired.

Kathy's shrug was as oddly adult as her frown. "He says he needs Christmas like he needs a case of the flu. And that it's nothing but a damn waste of time and... and...ah...espense!" She beamed at Kate with pride for having managed the unfamiliar word.

Kate felt a sharp catch in her throat and her heart; she had never even laid eyes on the man, but she disliked him immensely! Kathy had to be *the* brightest child Kate had ever encountered, and the fool that had fathered her was not only teaching her to curse, he was robbing her of one of the joys of childhood! At that instant, Kate longed for the opportunity to give the insensitive brute a large piece of her mind, along with the sharp edge of her tongue!

"What's espense mean?" Kathy's question shattered Kate's vision of a certain male's chastisement.

"The word is *ex*pense, darling," Kate explained softly. "And it means to cost a lost of money."

"My daddy has a lot of money," Kathy said seriously. "Lots and lots of pennies...and even quarters!"

"That's nice, love." Kate's smile was tinged with genuine amusement; how simplistic children were, equating wealth with lots and lots of pennies and even quarters!

And it had required quite a few of those quarters to outfit the child, Kate decided, running an encompassing glance over Kathy's sturdy figure as they stood in the midst of the hubbub of shoppers.

The child's snowsuit alone had very likely been exorbitantly expensive. Beneath the open jacket, Kate could see and evaluate the cost of the luxurious velour smock and corduroy slacks the girl was wearing. The supple furlined, leather boots encasing her tiny feet hadn't come from a bargain counter either!

At least the absent parent was scrupulous in the child's physical well-being, Kate conceded grudgingly. But that certainly didn't compensate for his dereliction of duty as far as the girl's emotional security was concerned. And, if anyone had firsthand knowledge of the lack of emotional security, Kate did!

"I'm hungry, Kate." Kathy's whimper drew Kate away from the unpleasant memory of her own barren childhood.

"Are you?" At the girl's nod, Kate asked, "Didn't you have any lunch?"

Kathy's blond curls bounced on her shoulders with a negative shake of her head. "Daddy said I could have a hamburger and French fries at McDonald's." Her lower lip quivered, "And now daddy's lost, and I'm hungry."

Her gaze was captured by the trembling rosebud mouth, and Kate sighed in defeat. Oh, well, she'd simply have to explain the whole thing to David later—surely he'd understand why she'd had to stand him up. But to be honest, Kate wasn't all that positive that he *would* understand; David had been displaying an uncomfortable tendency toward possessiveness lately.

Pushing thoughts of the man waiting to have lunch with her from her mind, Kate grinned at Kathy.

"You know what? I'm hungry too." Tightening her hold on the child's hand, Kate walked determinedly in the direction of the mall office. "So, let's go tell the authorities that your daddy is lost, and where we're going, and then we'll both have a hamburger and French fries at McDonald's. Okay?"

"Okay!" Kathy agreed, smiling all over her adorable little face.

Some thirty-odd minutes later, Kate and Kathy were ensconced in a booth inside the fast-food restaurant, happily munching on Big Macs and golden slices of deep-fried potatoes, washing it down with large cups of cola.

Though Kate had hoped that she and Kathy would find the negligent parent pacing the mall office, she had to admit that she wasn't devastated that they hadn't. In fact, she had to admit that she was having a great time with the intelligent little girl.

Endearingly at ease now with Kate, Kathy rambled on about how she was going to see Santa Claus, even though her disgruntled father was vocal with disapproval, and that afterward she was going to visit her grandparents for the rest of the weekend.

"You like visiting your grandparents, don't you?" Kate asked, knowing the answer by the gleam in Kathy's eyes.

"Uh huh," Kathy nodded vigorously. "Gramma plays games with me, and grampa takes me for long walks." She chewed methodically a moment then added wistfully, "Sometimes my mommie is there—" she sighed "—and then everybody just yells a lot."

Kate felt an actual stab of pain in her chest at the too-wise expression on the youngster's face. Back off of this subject, Katie my girl, she advised herself ruefully. Still, she couldn't help but deplore how people managed to tangle up their lives and hurt their children in the process.

"Ah...what are you going to tell Santa Claus?" she asked with forced brightness. "What do you want him to bring you for Christmas?"

"A new mommie," Kathy said emphatically, stunning Kate into stillness for several seconds.

"But—" Kate shook her head "—but, Kathy, you already have a mommie! Why do you want a new one?" Kate blurted out without thinking.

"That is none of your damned business!"

Kate jumped at the harsh male voice coming from behind her left shoulder. Shifting around on the plastic-covered booth seat, she found herself staring into glacial green eyes just as Kathy squealed:

"Daddy!"

A chill invaded Kate's spine as she gazed into the harshly etched face of the cold-eyed man. *This* was Kathy's father? Instantly the image Kate had formed of the man dissolved: this man was definitely not a swaggering young macho-man. Oh no, this man exuded an aura of arrogant self-confidence that was so palpable that Kate fancied she could feel its rays enveloping her, smothering her with their force.

In a mere moment that seemed to last forever, the man's entire appearance was impressed upon Kate's mind and memory.

He was not exceptionally tall, perhaps an inch under six foot, yet every one of those five feet eleven inches was solidly packed with large, angular bones covered tautly with lean, hard-looking muscles. He was attired in a casual, ordinary fashion—tan brushed-denim jeans, a dark brown-and-white striped bulky knit sweater, desert boots and a Western-style, sheepskin-lined jacket, both in buff suede. On him the clothes looked neither casual nor ordinary!

But it was his facial features that caused the chill in Kate's spine to spread insidiously through her entire body. Made up of hard angles and smooth planes encased in wind- and sun-roughened skin, nose long and straight, cheekbones wide and high, jaw line uncompromisingly hard, all framed by a thick mane of chestnut-shaded hair, he was devestatingly handsome in a thoroughly masculine, almost brutal, way.

The mere sight of him scared Kate! But, of course, she had no intention of allowing *him* to see it!

"You're Kathy's father?" Kate infused a hint of contempt into her cool tone.

"That's right," he snapped, moving to stand beside the bright-eyed child. "Who the hell are you?"

Heat raced through Kate's veins, and she felt a surge of warmth rush into her cheeks at his insulting tone. Of all the ungrateful…! Kate's mind groped for words strong enough to indict the brute and went blank in the process. Never before in her life had she encountered such arrogance!

"*I* am the woman who has been looking after your daughter," Kate gritted furiously. "The one *you* mislaid!"

His narrowing eyes spoke of his own rising anger. "*I* mislaid? I'll have you know—" he began roughly when Kathy cut in excitedly.

"Daddy, this is Kate, she was helping me find you when you got lost!"

"I got lost?" he exclaimed incredulously. "Young lady, I told you to stay beside me while I paid for your shoes!" The hard-eyed stare he leveled on Kathy aroused Kate's maternal instincts, but before she could voice a protest, he went on icily, "Get your jacket, we're leaving."

"But, daddy," Kathy cried, "I just started—"

"And you're not seeing Santa Claus today," he cut in brusquely.

Kate gasped, stunned by his cruelty. But when she saw the large tears welling up in Kathy's eyes, she flung caution to the wind and, regaining her voice, she launched into a defensive attack.

"Your behavior is unforgivable, *sir*!" Kate sneered the term of respect. "Kathy has barely started her lunch!"

"The name is Sinclair," he said much too softly. "Trace Sinclair." A chilling smile twisted his lips. "But you may call me sir." An arctic stare was raked over what he could see of Kate's body, lingering an insulting moment on her high, full breasts. Then, dismissively, he turned his attention back to his daughter.

"Daddy, I'm hungry!" Kathy wailed pleadingly. "Can't I finish my hamburger and French fries?"

Her blood near the boiling point, Kate bit her tongue against the tirade choking her and glared at his profile, willing him to show the child patience and compassion. When he relented, Kate knew it was because of the tears now running freely down Kathy's flushed cheeks, and not from her silent urging.

"All right," Trace Sinclair said abruptly, "I did promise you lunch at McDonald's." His less than enthusiastic glance swept over the food in front of Kathy. "And, since I have to wait for you," he sighed, "I may as well eat too."

Kate aimed visual daggers at his back as he swung away to stride to the order counter. The man was an absolute tyrant, she thought, trembling with anger. What sort of life must this poor baby have? Her fighting spirit awakened, Kate was determined that Kathy would see Santa

Claus after lunch even if she had to make an embarrass-
ing scene to bring the visit about!

"Why is daddy mad at me, Kate?" Kathy's tremulous
voice drew Kate from her fuming thoughts.

Withdrawing a tissue from her handbag, Kate reached
across the narrow table to wipe the tears from the small
face. "I'm sure your daddy was more worried than angry, darling," Kate smiled reassuringly, not particularly
assured herself. "I suppose that when he was lost, your
daddy was afraid you wouldn't be able to find him."

"My daddy's not afraid of anything!" Kathy blurted,
wide-eyed. "Not even snakes and crawly things!"

"Really?" Kate contrived a note of awe.

"Yes, really." Trace's drawl surprised Kate. She hadn't
noticed him approaching the booth. "Not snakes or
crawly things or anything else." A mocking smile curved
his hard-looking lips, "Not even afraid of intrepid young
rescuers of disobedient children." His eyes gleamed as he
noted Kate's soft gasp. "May I join you, Miss...?" One
dark eyebrow arched tauntingly.

"Kate," Kathy volunteered.

"Warren," Kate said repressively. "And please do,"
she waved a negligent hand regally, "join us, I mean."

"How gracious," he murmured in a near growl before
slanting a glance at Kathy to order, "Slide it over, kid."

Kate's heart ached for the child as her expression
brightened at the teasing note in her father's tone. How
very little it takes to make her happy, Kate sighed inwardly, watching as Kathy scooted to the end of the
bench seat, her face glowing with a delighted smile.
Shifting her gaze, Kate silently renewed her vow to see
Kathy sit on Santa's lap as she observed Trace place his
food-laden tray on the table. He then shrugged out of his
jacket and eased onto the seat beside the child.

"So, *Kate*," he drawled, his taunting tone underlining her name. "Where did you run into my wandering offspring?"

Kate didn't even realize she was gritting her teeth until her jaw began to ache. "Gazing wide-eyed at the tree," Kate somehow managed to drawl back. "Right in the center of the mall," she paused, then added sweetly, "*Trace*."

A brief flicker in the eyes that Kate could now see were a clear light green acknowledged her deliberate use of his first name. "Not thirty feet from the store where we had just purchased her shoes..." he shot a grim glance at Kathy, "...while I was frantically searching the entire mall." His features hardening, Trace caught the child's tiny chin in his strong hand and lifted her head to face him directly. "If you ever walk away from me like that again, Kath, I'll tan your rear with my belt. Do you understand?"

"Yes, daddy."

The quiver in Kathy's voice and the wounded expression that seemed to crumble her face sent a bolt of sheer rage through Kate. In her mind's eye a vision rose of Trace wielding a belt on the beautiful child, and common sense gave way to her protective urges.

"Over my dead body!" Kate exclaimed in a grating tone.

An uncommon stillness gripped Trace, then he slowly turned his head to pierce her with glittering green eyes. "I beg your pardon?" he murmured ominously.

"I said, the only way you'll ever take a belt to this child is over my dead body!" Kate reiterated, incensed and not thinking rationally. "I'll see you in hell first!"

Amazement transformed Trace's features for an instant, then a curtain was drawn, concealing emotion—

except in his eyes. A contemplative watchfulness gave his eyes a gemlike gleam.

"Indeed?" His food ignored as if forgotten, Trace regarded Kate with cool consideration. "And how do you propose to carry out this ferocious guardianship?" he gibed in a deceptively soft tone.

Stark awareness shuddered through Kate, not only of her inability to back up her hastily blurted challenge, but of an uncomfortable sexual awareness of Trace as a man. All kinds of sensations went zigzagging through her body, leaving her hot and cold at the same time. Her breathing was suddenly shallow and painful and she stared at Trace helplessly.

Immune to the electric force field of currents shimmering between the two adults, Kathy's plaintive interruption shattered the raw intimacy humming between Trace and Kate.

"Daddy, please, please let me see Santa Claus today," she whined, sniffing loudly. "You promised!"

"That's very good." Drawing his gaze from Kate reluctantly, Trace smiled wryly at Kathy. Kathy returned the smile sheepishly. A frown line marring her smooth brow, Kate glanced from father to daughter in confusion; Trace's follow-up observation clarified his seemingly unrelated remark...at least partially.

"You're becoming quite the little con-artist with your begging routine; you should take the show on the road." His lips flattened into a forbidding straight line. "Picked that little whining number up from your cousins, did you?" he demanded coldly.

Kathy hung her head abjectly. "Yeah."

"Excuse me?" Trace rapped at her terminology.

"Yes, daddy," Kathy corrected.

Removed from the exchange, Kate continued to shift her glance from one to the other. From what she could gather, Kathy was acquiring some habits from relatives that Trace firmly objected to.

"Maybe your Aunt Barbara and Uncle Fred will put up with your cousins' behavior," Trace continued, confirming Kate's speculation, "but I certainly will not." His tone hardened, "Is *that* understood, Kath?"

"Yes, daddy," Kathy whispered.

"All right." Lifting her head with one long finger, Trace smiled so gently at her that it caused a dry tightness in Kate's throat. "Now finish your lunch," he ordered softly, "before it gets completely cold."

Silence blanketed the table for the following fifteen minutes as the three concentrated on their food. Kate utilized those minutes devising ways to change Trace's mind about Kathy's visit to Santa Claus, studying her adversary from the protection of her lowered eyelashes.

And Trace Sinclair did make an interesting study! The first descriptive word that sprang to Kate's mind was arrogant—swiftly followed by self-confident, rugged, virile, and supremely male.

Feeling uneasy by the strange, new sensations whirling through her body, Kate shifted on the seat. Through the veil of her thick black lashes, her gaze touched then became caught on the thin masculine lips. His lips moved as he murmured something to his daughter, and a sigh of longing to feel those lips moving on hers shivered through Kate.

The longing, spawned from blatant sexual hunger, shocked Kate to the marrow of her delicate bones. What in the world was happening to her, she wondered, frantically shifting her gaze away from temptation. Never in her life had she experienced such a strong physical attraction to a man!

Clutching the paper cup of cola with trembling, achy fingers, Kate gulped at the cold liquid in a futile attempt to quench the flames of desire licking her senses into hot arousal. Observing her trembling fingers as if they belonged to someone else, she felt a sinking feeling in her stomach.

Did those fingers really belong to the woman who had earned herself the title of "the unresponsive one" while she was still in college? How many frustrated men had called her that? Kate had lost count of the number. Yet, now, sitting in a public place with a man she'd met less than an hour ago, she found herself responding to everything male in him.

What was happening to her? With the silent cry ringing in her mind, Kate exerted every ounce of willpower she possessed in an effort to appear coolly composed as she raised her eyes. The heat in the eyes that met hers sent a delicious tingle of sheer anticipation skittering along her spine.

Good Lord! A man could lose his soul in the depths of those smoldering smoky-gray eyes!

A rush of hot desire swept through his body as Trace stared, with a sudden intense hunger, into the eyes of his daughter's beautiful champion.

And Kate Warren was beautiful...breathtakingly so! Not even bothering with the effort of concealment, Trace devoured Kate's face and form with a fiery gaze, from the riot of gleaming black waves that fell softly to her shoulders to the narrow waist he could discern just below the table edge. And every luscious inch revealed during his inspection made his lips ache with the need to explore the inviting satin skin hiding under her clothes.

Shaken by the intensity of the desire raging inside his mind and body, Trace frowned fiercely at the woman who'd created the blaze.

What was it about Kate that had sent his libido into overdrive, he railed irritably. So she was beautiful with all that silky black hair he ached to dig his fingers into. So she was alluring with enticing smoky-gray eyes surrounded by unbelievably long, thick lashes set in a patricianly boned face he longed to touch. So she was sexually exciting with that slender, delicately wrought body with gently sloping shoulders and high full breasts he burned to imprint with his own angular strength.

So what? He knew many women with equally beautiful faces, enticing eyes and exciting bodies. Why then, Trace brooded, did he feel he had to possess this one woman above all others?

Merely admitting the compelling need to himself made Trace uncomfortable. Damn it! The last thing on earth he wanted was to feel a *need* for anybody...especially for a woman. The disintegration of his marriage and subsequent desertion of his wife had cured him of the ills of *needing* another person.

At least Trace had convinced himself he'd been cured. In the four years since his wife had walked out of their home, Trace had experienced countless hours and situations during which his body had tormented him with the demand for physical release.

Imposing a will forged out of the fire of devastated pride into the tempered steel of determination, Trace had ruthlessly denied the demands of his body, submerging them in the celibacy that had begun with Kathy's birth.

Never again, he'd vowed, would he allow his emotions to dictate to his mind. And, until now, Trace had steadfastly adhered to that vow.

Actually trembling, as much from his thoughts as from the passion searing his body, Trace stared into her smoky-gray eyes and cursed the circumstances that had brought him into contact with Kate Warren.

Reminded of those circumstances, Trace relived the stark fear he'd felt with the realization that Kathy had disappeared from his side. Slanting a glance at the child, he allowed himself the luxury of a sigh of relief. This tiny, exquisite daughter of his was the one and only person in the world that Trace loved. If he lost Kathy...Trace angrily pushed the consideration from his mind, unwilling to even think of it.

In a toss-up between remembered panic and renewed passion, Trace opted for the latter, sliding a thoughtful glance over Kate's delectable body. A twitch of a smile lifted the corners of his lips as he heard again the outrage in her tone when she issued her challenging statement "Over my dead body!"

Strange, he mused, how very protective she was of a child she barely knew. But, then, Kathy *was* an exceptionally attractive, bright child, with the ability to wrap all kinds of people around her small finger.

Trace grimaced inwardly, qualifying, all kinds of people except her own mother.

Bitterness ran as hot as passion through Trace's veins. Damn all women and their lack of integrity!

Deciding at that moment to get away from Kate as soon as decently possible, Trace narrowed his eyes when she once again had the temerity to question his authority.

"If you don't want to take Kathy to see Santa Claus, Trace," she said hesitantly, "would you have any objections if *I* took her?"

Kate's tone told Trace clearly that she fully expected him to refuse. And, in truth, he fully expected to. When he answered, it was hard to judge who was more surprised.

"I'll take Kathy to sit on Santa's lap, Kate," Trace stunned himself with his reply. "But you may come with us if you like."

Two

How did I get into this?"

Slanting a glance at Trace out of the corner of her eye, Kate hid a smile behind a manufactured cough and made believe that she hadn't heard his complaint. When her expression was once again serene, she surveyed the cause of his impatience.

The line of children waiting to chat with Santa Claus was very long and very noisy. And, as they'd arrived on the scene mere moments ago, Kathy was near the end of that long, noisy line.

Flanking Kathy on either side, Kate and Trace moved in unison as the line advanced one child length.

"I hope you had no plans for this afternoon, Kate," Trace said mockingly over Kathy's head. "At the rate this line is moving, we're liable to be here until dinnertime."

"I'd planned to do a little shopping," Kate admitted calmly. "But I can do that another time."

"Can Kate have dinner with us, daddy?" Kathy gazed up at her father imploringly. "Please?"

Kate's cheeks grew warm at the flash of annoyance that sparked Trace's eyes. "I'm sure Kate has a previous engagement, Kath," he said coolly. "Am I correct, Kate?" Raising his head, he challenged her with a glittering green stare.

That Trace couldn't wait to be rid of her was more than obvious. And she was equally anxious to get away from him, Kate assured herself firmly. But a retaliatory, devilish imp took control of her tongue.

"Actually, I'm free this afternoon." Kate smiled gently, relishing the flush that crept up over Trace's rocklike jaw. Your move, Mr. Sinclair, she thought wryly, amused by the telltale narrowing of his eyes.

"You're free to spend the rest of the afternoon *and* the evening with us?" Trace baited the trap so casually that Kate walked into it without a care or thought.

"Yes, I am." She smiled tauntingly, confident that she wouldn't have to break her date with David. Her confidence ebbed as Trace began to smile.

"Good." The softness of his tone gave it the distinct sound of a purr. His smile twisted warningly.

A warning tingle trailed down Kate's spine.

"I detest shopping." Plunging a hand into his pocket, Trace produced a crumpled piece of paper. "Women are so much more efficient at this sort of thing." He held the slip of paper out to her. Frowning her confusion, Kate automatically accepted it. "That's my Christmas list." Now the smile that had lifted the corners of his lips was almost feral.

"You want me to do your Christmas shopping for you?" Kate asked blankly, once again moving in unison with him as the line advanced.

Trace nodded decisively, "In exchange for dinner—at the restaurant of your choice, of course."

Kate could have happily hit him; he was so smug! A cutting refusal sprang to her tongue. As if sensing what was coming, Kathy tugged on her skirt. Her lips tightly compressed, Kate glanced down at the child impatiently and immediately felt the fight drain out of her seeing the pleading expression in the round, innocent blue eyes.

"Please, Kate," Kathy begged, "it'll be fun."

Berating herself for a fool, Kate swallowed the refusal. Sighing in defeat, she managed a gentle smile for the child, mentally echoing Trace's earlier complaint of "How did I get into this?"

"I can't possibly do this all by myself." Ignoring the disgustingly complacent expression Trace was wearing, Kate stooped to Kathy's level. "You're going to have to help me with this," she waved the shopping list under the girl's button nose.

"Oh, yes!" Kathy enthused. "I know just what I want to get for everybody!"

And I hope every single purchase is enormously expensive, Kate thought sourly, raising her eyes to glare at Trace.

By the laughter dancing in the green gaze Kate encountered, it was quite evident that Trace was neither intimidated nor impressed. It also quickly became obvious that he read her intent with amazing accuracy.

"Planning to relieve me of a good deal of the weight in my wallet, are you?" he chided softly as Kate straightened.

"It will be a pleasure," Kate assured him sweetly.

If Kate had expected any response at all, it certainly wasn't the warm laughter that rippled from his throat, stabbing at a soft spot in the vicinity of her heart. Her

breath catching in her throat, she glanced away quickly
to hide her reaction. Fortunately at that moment the line
moved again, and Kate was surprised to see Kathy walk
confidently up to the man decked out in red velvet and
white fur.

When had the line advanced, she wondered, observing Kathy as she conversed animatedly with Santa. Kate
saw the man frown, then say something to the child.
Whatever he told Kathy, it must have been what she
wanted to hear for a glow sparkled in her eyes, and her
face lit up brighter than the huge tree behind Santa's
chair. Feeling ridiculous for her reaction, yet powerless
to prevent it, Kate felt her throat grow tight and her eyes
become misty at the sight of that happy little face. As she
slipped off of his lap, Kathy waved gaily.

"What a shame life robs us of that innocence."

Startled by the bitterness in Trace's tone, Kate looked
at him sharply, then wished she hadn't. His face appeared locked up, devoid of all expression, and fright-
ening because of the absence of emotion.

This man has been very badly hurt. For some obscure
reason Kate wasn't even tempted to examine, the realization of Trace's vulnerability touched that same soft
spot in her heart.

"Trace?" All the compassion that Kate held within
was contained in that solitary word. Trace rejected it with
a cold stare.

"Save the maternal understanding for Kath," he
snarled under his breath, stretching out a hand for his
approaching daughter. "I don't need or want it."

"That was neat!"

Kathy's excitedly high-pitched voice covered the gasp
that escaped Kate's lips at his unbending tone. Had she
really felt sympathy for him for an instant? How posi-

tively naive of her. The man was as vulnerable as a spitting tiger.

"So, did you give the old boy your list of gimmes?" Trace teased Kathy in a chiding drawl.

"I only asked for one thing," Kathy replied seriously.

"My bank balance rejoices." Trace grinned. "Or is that one thing going to wipe me out financially?"

"I don't think so." Kathy frowned. "But, even if it does, it'll be worth it."

"To whom?" Trace retorted.

"To me, acourse." Amazingly, Kathy's grin mirrored her father's.

Her gaze flashing from one to the other, Kate could only stare, transfixed by the exchange. She had realized almost at once that the little girl was very bright, but now Kate had the odd sensation she was listening to a miniature adult. Except for the occasional mispronunciation, Kathy's vocabulary was as good if not better than some teenagers Kate knew, and the intelligence she displayed was that of a much older child.

"Don't let it throw you, Kate." The softly drawled advice indicated that Trace had correctly read her reaction again. "Kath has been around adults for every one of her four years. But your thinking is on target. She is an exceptionally bright child."

"Four!" Kate looked at Kathy closely. "I'd have thought she was less than three."

"Her mother is very small—" Trace grimaced "—and delicate."

"And she has blond hair, just like me," Kathy piped in.

"Ah...that's nice, honey." Feeling out of her depth, and going down for the third time, Kate gazed helplessly into the child's innocent blue eyes. There were currents here that she had no desire to get caught up in, yet she could already feel the tug of the undertow. And, if she was being completely honest with herself, Kate knew that the tug came as strongly from the rough-voiced man beside her as from the sweet-faced child she was gazing at.

"So, are we going to shop, or are we going to stand here blocking traffic?"

Jarred from her uncomfortable introspection by that same rough-voiced man, Kate pulled herself together and forced a smile for Kathy.

"We're going to shop," she declared, winking at the smiling child. "Right, baby?"

"Right." Kathy nodded her head vigorously.

"Kathy is not a baby." The flat statement was issued from a frowning Trace as they strolled away from the milling youngsters. "As far as that goes," he continued instructively, "Kathy was never called 'baby' even when she was an infant."

Kate felt her face grow warm for the second time in one hour. Embarrassed, she smiled ruefully at the girl.

"I'm sorry, Kathy!" Kate wasn't sure if she was sorry for having called the child "baby," or for the fact that no one ever had.

"I'm not!" Kathy yelped. "I like it!"

Unable to resist, Kate tossed a superior glance at Trace before laughing down at the child. "I'm glad, because *I* like it too."

The only response Trace made sounded suspiciously like a snort. Grinning unrepentantly at each other, Kate and Kathy clasped hands as they entered the first of many stores.

Some three and a half hours later, Trace called a halt to the frenzy of shopping Kate and Kathy had indulged

in. Hands planted on his hips, he scowled at the two females.

"I've had it." His tone brooked no arguments. "I'm
tired of the crowds. I'm tired of the pushing and shoving. I'm tired, period." His eyebrows drew together as if
warning either child or woman not to voice a protest.
"I'm hungry, and I need a drink." A long-suffering sigh
moved his chest, "In fact, I need several drinks." He indicated the exit doors with an imperious wave of his
hand. "Move out." Trace bit the order out tersely.

"Yes, sir!" Straightening her spine and squaring her
shoulders, Kate pivoted on her heel and marched toward
the doors, Kathy's muffled squeal of laughter following
her.

Kate remembered her date with David as she marched
past the bank of phones near the exit. Spinning around,
she held up her palm like a traffic officer.

"I have to make a call," she explained, rooting in her
bag for her wallet. Before her fingers made contact with
her change purse, a hand was extended to her. "Thank
you," she murmured, accepting the coin Trace offered.

"Kath and I will go get the car. We'll pick you up out
front in a few minutes." Grasping Kathy's hand he strode
off.

Strange man, Kate mused, studying his retreating back.
After the way he'd spoken to her when they'd met, then
manipulated her into doing his shopping for him, the
very last thing Kate had expected from Trace Sinclair was
sensitivity to her need for privacy while making her phone
call.

Shrugging, Kate dropped the coin into the box and
dialed David's number. Breaking her date with him
wasn't going to be easy, especially with the pangs of guilt

that were already stabbing her conscience. David didn't make it any easier.

"What!" he shouted after she'd explained she couldn't go out with him. Holding the receiver away from her ear, Kate winced as he continued. "What do you mean, you have to break our date? And where were you at lunchtime?" he went on angrily before she could answer. "I waited an hour and a half for you!"

"I *am* sorry, David," Kate said contritely. "But, you see, I ran into this little girl who was lost, and I simply couldn't leave her standing all alone and frightened."

"Well, why didn't you take her to the mall office? They'd have kept her until her parents showed up." Exasperation sharpened David's voice.

"I did take her to the office," Kate explained patiently. "But her—" She caught herself just in time. Biting back the word father, Kate began again. "But there was no one there for her and she was hungry, so I took her to lunch. I knew you'd understand," she finished quickly.

"Well, I'm sorry, but I don't," he snapped. "The kid was not your responsibility."

Suddenly Kate's guilty feeling gave way to anger. She hated the way he said the word kid! Odd, but she hadn't minded at all when Trace had called his daughter that.

"I couldn't leave her, David." Kate repeated grittily.

"Okay, you couldn't leave her," David sighed his frustration. "But what has that got to do with our date tonight?"

"I...ah..." Careful, Kate, she cautioned. "I've been invited to have dinner with her as a reward." Closing her eyes, Kate prayed for forgiveness.

"Oh, come on, Kate!" David was obviously at the end of his limited supply of patience. "Why didn't you simply accept a check and say a polite goodbye?"

"I couldn't accept money for staying with Kathy!" Kate protested on a gasp.

"Why not, for heaven's sake?" David demanded. "It's done all the time."

"Not by me," Kate shot back. "Kathy is an adorable little girl, David. I spent the entire afternoon with her, and I loved every minute of it." Well, perhaps not *every* minute, she qualified silently, remembering several sticky moments with Trace. "And I have agreed to have dinner with her," she continued adamantly. "I'm not sure why, but I gather that she's not from around here, so I'll probably never see her again."

"And you can see me anytime. Is that it?" David grumbled.

Not if you whine more than a four-year-old, Kate advised him mentally. A flashing image of a moment at lunch brought a smile to her eyes and a retort to her lips.

"That crushed act is very good, David," she paraphrased Trace. "Perhaps you ought to take it on the road."

There was a tense silence for a few moments, as if David was holding his breath. And, when he finally responded there was a breathless quality to his voice.

"Are you trying to tell me something?"

Not wanting to hurt him, Kate had agonized for weeks over how to break off their one-sided relationship. Now, thoroughly disgusted with his childish possessiveness, she drew a deep breath and ended it.

"Yes, David, I am. I've tried to tell you before that I don't want a deeper relationship with you."

"Kate, listen—"

"No, David, not this time," Kate cut him off ruthlessly. "You've applied too much pressure, much too quickly. I'm not ready for that kind of involvement. I'm sorry, David. Goodbye."

Kate replaced the receiver gently, then turned to hurry through the exit to the car that waited opposite the doors.

The passenger door was hanging open, Kathy was ensconced in the back seat, and Trace was at the back of the car, ready to stash the bulging shopping bag Kate was carrying into the already crowded trunk. Walking up to him, she silently held the bag out.

"Trouble with your call?" Trace searched her face as he relieved her of the bag.

"No!" Aware of the abruptness of her response, Kate managed an unconvincing smile. "No, of course not. Why do you ask?"

Trace didn't return the smile, "Because you have the same rebellious expression Kath gets when things don't go her way." His glance lowered to her lips. "The same pouty look to your mouth, too."

"I don't pout, Mr...." Kate forgot what she was saying. Her breath growing shallow, she watched a light flare in his eyes as his gaze clung to her now trembling lips.

"Strange," he mused, slowly, reluctantly raising his eyes to hers. "When Kath gets that look, I have to fight the urge to reprimand her. On you, that pouty look produces an altogether different urge."

"What?" Kate could barely breathe, let alone speak. The sensual expression that softened his rugged features dried every bit of moisture in her mouth and throat.

"You know very well...what." Trace arched one brow mockingly. His voice went very low and disturbingly sexy. "And, at some point before this evening's over, I fully intend to indulge that urge."

"I...I think not," Kate muttered, moving away from him.

"Think again," Trace advised adamantly, slamming the trunk lid for emphasis.

Buckled into the bucket seat beside Trace, Kate's imagination ran rampant with speculation. At the same time, her blood rushed through her veins and pounded loudly in her temples.

Trace meant that before the night was over he was going to kiss her. Well, that was nothing to get bent out of shape about—was it? Of course not, Kate assured herself. She'd been kissed before—many times. No big deal. But, suppose he'd meant something else? Biting her lip, Kate gave Trace a swift sideways glance. What else could he have meant? Who are you kidding, she chided herself. His expression, combined with the way his eyes had seemed to darken, had definitely been what is commonly referred to as that "bedroom" look. A streak of something she refused to identify as excitement flashed through Kate. Good grief! Was she crazy? She didn't even know the man!

"Where are we going to eat, daddy?"

Kate sighed with relief as Kathy's question snapped the tension singing along her nerves. Waiting for his reply, she turned in her seat to look at Trace and immediately wished she hadn't.

Reflecting her thoughts, Trace's lips curved sensuously. The gaze he quickly ran over her ignited flash fires all over her body. "It's up to Kate," he finally answered. "I told her she could choose the restaurant."

"Kate?" Kathy nudged.

Shifting around as far as she could within the confines of the seat belt, Kate smiled at Kathy. "It really doesn't matter to me, honey. Is there somewhere special that you'd like to go?''

"No," Kathy shook her head. "We don't know too many places around here," she confided, reinforcing Kate's hunch that they were not local residents. "We've only been to one fancy restaurant and a pizza place."

Kate caught the wistful note in Kathy's voice as she mentioned the latter establishment. She also caught the smile that eased Trace's lips as he shot Kathy a warning glance in the rearview mirror. The warning said: this is Kate's choice.

"Pizza is fine with me," Kate laughed, amazed at the level of silent communication between father and daughter.

"Where are you two from?" Kate had held her curiosity at bay until they were seated in a booth at the restaurant.

"Texas," Kathy said proudly.

"Outside San Antonio," Trace supplemented.

"I thought I detected a drawl." Kate smiled at Kathy. "I just couldn't decide whether it was of the southern or western variety." Turning to Trace, she probed, "You're a rancher?"

His soft laughter did strange and wonderful things to her equilibrium. "Why do all easterners imagine that all Texans are ranchers?" Trace grinned, "Even Texans need medical help on occasion."

"You're a doctor?" Kate blurted out artlessly.

"Blows your mind, does it?"

Avoiding his mocking eyes, Kate studied the flickering candle on the table. A doctor! Kate hadn't the vaguest idea why it should, but the information *did* blow her mind! Trace Sinclair simply looked too earthy to be a physician.

"Daddy's a very good doctor, Kate." Kathy's aggrieved tone snagged Kate's attention.

"I'm sure he is, honey," she soothed before returning her gaze to Trace. "Do you specialize?"

"I'm a neurosurgeon, Kate." Observing her with eyes gleaming in amusement, Trace waited for a reaction to his coolly intoned statement. He didn't have to wait long.

"Oh!" Kate's mouth and eyes opened simultaneously. His roar of laughter brought her to her senses. "I'm sorry." Kate's smile was sheepish. "I didn't mean to be rude. It's just that—" she shrugged helplessly "—you don't look like a doctor, let alone a neurosurgeon!"

"Really?" Trace frowned mockingly. "What exactly does a neurosurgeon look like?"

"I...I don't know." Kate searched her mind for a way out of her dilemma. Trace's movement as he raised his beer mug to his lips caught her attention. "You do have the hands of a surgeon."

Trace was off again, his rich, rumbling laughter drawing reciprocal smiles from Kathy and the other patrons in the restaurant. "Oh, Kate!" Pausing to catch his breath, Trace shook his head, "You're a gem. I can't remember the last time I laughed like that." His gleaming eyes danced with amusement as he watched the flush tinge her cheeks dark pink. "How would you like to come back to Texas with me?" Kate's gasp went unheard as he continued, "You'd be just the person to come home to after long, grueling hours in the operating room."

She was being teased and she knew it, yet she had to hold back on the automatic "yes" that sprang to her lips. Stunned by her uncharacteristic, spontaneous response to Trace *and* his ridiculous offer, she stared at him through eyes that betrayed her desire. Distracted with trying to figure out her own conflicting emotions, Kate was blind to the light of hope flaring in his eyes.

For the length of a heartbeat, their entire attention centered on each other's eyes. Trace and Kate were beyond noticing another pair of eyes, sparkling blue, set in a small intense face.

"Come to Texas, Kate." Trace broke the visual thread binding her to him.

Blinking herself back to reality, Kate glanced around the room, as if wondering where she was and how she'd gotten there. Never before had she experienced the sensation of being lost inside a man's compelling gaze, and this particular man's eyes held the allure of a cool, green glade on a hot summer day.

"Oh, yes, please, Kate! Come with us to Texas!" The high-pitched excitement in Kathy's young voice tugged at Kate's heartstrings.

"But that's impossible, baby!" The light laugh Kate attempted didn't quite come off.

"Why?" Kathy's rosebud lips curved down in disappointment.

"Honey, you must understand. I have a job here, responsibilities, a family! I can't simply uproot myself. I..." Kate's voice trailed away and she shrugged. Who was she hoping to convince, she taunted herself. Kathy and Trace Sinclair, or Kate Warren?

"What do you do, Kate?" Trace asked in a tone devoid of inflection.

"Do?" Kate frowned her confusion revealingly.

Not unaware of his effect on women, Trace smiled. "You said you have a job. What sort of job?"

"Oh!" Kate shook her head at her own incredulous density—what *was* wrong with her, anyway? "I'm an insurance rater," she finally managed.

"Ah, yes," Trace drawled. "I've dealt with a few insurance raters."

Kate winced. She didn't need a code book to decipher his sardonic tone. She was in a position to know the enormity of the current malpractice insurance rates.

"I'm...I'm sorry." Kate sighed. How many times had she apologized since meeting him? *That* was another new experience!

"What for?" The gentle smile that curved his lips shook Kate to the very center of her being. "I didn't think you were personally responsible for the rates."

"What are you talking about?" Kathy demanded, obviously put out at being excluded from the conversation.

"Nothing very interesting, kid." Reaching out, Trace ruffled her blond curls. "Where's our dinner?" He frowned ferociously, coaxing a giggle from Kathy. "I wouldn't want my best girl to fade away to a shadow!"

Suddenly feeling left out, Kate listened to the teasing banter exchanged by Trace and Kathy until the arrival of their meal ended it.

All through dinner, Kate mulled over her reaction to both the situation and the two people who'd precipitated it.

Along with the pungent aroma of spicy tomato sauce and garlic bread, her senses swam with the whirlpool of events she'd been caught up in since lunchtime.

Carefully twirling spaghetti onto a fork, Kate readily acknowledged that she'd completely lost her heart to the blue-eyed, blond child happily digging into a slice of pizza across the table from her. As to the man next to her,

Kate was ambivalent—a state which by itself was unsettling.

Observing Trace surreptitiously while sipping her glass of wine, Kate attempted to sort out her own conflicting emotions.

Most definitely there were more facets to his character than were apparent at their first meeting. Though certainly strong-willed and more than a little arrogant, Trace had revealed glimpses of a capacity for deep understanding and sensitivity as well. While owning his fair share of self-confidence, he'd shown moments of uncertainty and doubt. As if he could not bear the sight of her, he had growled at her one minute, only to confound her the next by teasing her as gently as he did his obviously adored daughter.

How was a woman supposed to be anything *but* of two minds with such a complex man, Kate wondered, sighing softly.

"Is there something wrong with your food?" Trace asked, hearing her sigh and misinterpreting it.

"Not at all," Kate assured him, smiling to emphasize her words. "There is just too much of it!" She improvised the excuse. "And, wanting to set an example for our baby, I've been trying to clean my plate."

"Our baby?" Until Trace murmured the question for her ears alone, Kate wasn't even aware of her odd phrasing. Having it pointed out to her, even in a whisper, made her grow hot with embarrassment all over again.

"Our? Did I say our? I didn't mean to say our! Really, I meant *your* baby!" Kate was chattering, but she simply could not stop the flow of words. The slow smile lifting the edges of Trace's lips didn't help much either.

Casually leaning back in his chair, Trace slid an all-encompassing glance over Kate, then Kathy, then Kate

again. As if he'd come to an important decision, he nodded once.

"Kathy's beautiful," he said in that same low tone. "But, we'd make an equally beautiful child together."

Kate gave fervent thanks that she was sitting down because if she hadn't been, she'd have collapsed from the shock of his softly voiced assertion. The suggestion set loose a series of disturbingly exciting visions...every one of them erotic!

Swallowing to restore moisture to her suddenly parched throat, Kate chocked, "As chances are slim to none of that ever happening, we'll never know—will we?"

"Won't we?" Trace murmured before turning his attention to Kathy, who'd stopped eating to stare at them curiously. "Beginning to stall, Kath?" he asked blandly.

"Are you and Kate fighting in whispers?" Kathy demanded.

"Fighting? Kate and I?" Trace grinned, "Ridiculous!"

"Are you sure?" Unconvinced, Kathy's little face puckered into a frown.

His eyes bright with a devilish glow, Trace swung his gaze to Kate. "Are we fighting, Kate?" His tone was laced with contrived confusion.

The onus was now on her and Kate squirmed in her chair. The beast, she thought, exerting all her willpower to control the smile tugging at her lips. Trace Sinclair deserved a thorough shaking up! Allowing the smile free rein, she reached across the table to grasp Kathy's hand.

"Yes, we are fighting." Her smile flashed momentarily at Trace, then returned to the frowning child. "But, don't let it upset you, baby. It was only a word fight." She squeezed Kathy's hand gently to let her know she was only teasing. "You see, now that I know the rules of this

word game, I can beat your father at it with one lip tied down." As she finished, Kate winked at Kathy conspiratorially.

"She thinks!" Trace retorted, chuckling softly.

"Boy! This is fun!" Slipping her fingers from Kate's hand, Kathy clapped her palms together gleefully. "I really, really love you guys!"

Three

"Where have you been?"

Trace stiffened at the imperious demand in the voice that flung the question at him. His arms tightened reflexively around the sleeping child in his arms—his child, the single good out of a thoroughly bad marriage.

"I asked you a question!" Annette's voice rose impatiently.

"I heard you." Trace didn't raise his voice from a murmur, only his eyebrows went up—mockingly. "Do you think you could save the third degree until after our daughter is settled?" A shiver skipped the length of his spine as inside his head a soft voice echoed—wanting to set an example for our baby, I've been trying to clean my plate.

Turning abruptly, Trace mounted the open stairs in the ultramodern town house of his former in-laws. Annette's mother met him in the wide hallway.

"Let me help you with her, Trace." A gentle smile curved the older woman's lips as she preceded him into the room kept exclusively for Kathy.

Working swiftly and silently, they got Kathy out of her clothes and into her nightie without waking her. Trace brushed his lips over her soft pink cheek as he drew the covers up to her tiny chin, then followed her grandmother out of the room.

"Did you have a nice day?" Ruth asked softly as Trace quietly closed the door. "Did Kathy talk to Santa Claus?"

"Yes." Trace smiled at his daughter's grandmother, wondering, for perhaps the thousandth time, how she'd managed to produce a child so unlike herself. "We had a very nice day." A vision of a young, dark-haired beauty tantilized his memory and body. "And Kath did talk to Santa." A frown darkened his brow. "I'm sorry if I inconvenienced you by not having Kath back for dinner, Ruth." He shrugged. "She wanted pizza."

"I wasn't inconvenienced, Trace!" Ruth protested softly. "Regardless of what Annette might say to the contrary." A spasm of pain rippled across her still lovely face. "She's waiting for you. You'd better go down." Her narrow shoulders moved with the sigh of regret that lifted her chest. "I'm sorry, Trace." As she moved away from him towards her own bedroom, she whispered, "Sorry for everything."

His green eyes stormy with emotion, Trace watched as Ruth slipped inside her room before turning to the stairs and the confrontation waiting for him below.

Annette was standing in the center of the narrow living room, one tiny, slender foot tapping an impatient tune on the honey-colored hardwood floor.

His features locked into an expressionless mask, Trace sauntered into the room. Shrugging out of his jacket and tossing it onto a delicately wrought, satin-covered chair in gold and green stripes, he arched one eyebrow at her quizzically.

"Something bothering you, Annette?" Trace contained a smile of satisfaction at the frown his cooly unconcerned tone elicited from his former wife.

"Mother expected you to have Kathy back in time for dinner!" Annette's perfectly fashioned lips twisted over her daughter's name—a name she had resisted from the beginning and still detested. "She was very upset."

All too aware of how she felt, had *always* felt about bestowing his mother's name on their child, Trace narrowed his eyes warningly. "You're a liar," he said brutally. "I spoke to Ruth upstairs and she assured me she was not in the least upset." Moving into the room, he dropped lithely into a padded club chair. "You're up to something," he said disinterestedly. "Let's get it over with, Annette."

It was going to be bad, Trace knew it. His muscles tightened, he watched her closely, waiting for the verbal blow to fall. At that instant, Trace could have sworn he could feel the tension shimmering in her petite body.

"I'm seeing my attorney Monday, Trace." Annette's slim heels clicked as she moved to stand militantly in front of him.

"Good for you, or him, or whoever." Not by the slightest tremor did his tone betray the sudden clenching sensation Trace felt in his gut. "But what does that have to do with me?"

"You're so superior!" Annette hissed, her blue eyes flashing with hate. "Well, we'll see how damned superior you feel after you've lost custody of your precious child!"

Staring at the ugliness twisting her classically beautiful face, Trace felt suddenly sick to his stomach and cold to his very soul.

"You signed the papers nearly four years ago, Annette. You have never been a mother to Kathy." Trace leaned back into the chair with a deceptive ease; he'd die before showing weakness to this woman, or any other, ever again. "You can't take her from me."

Annette's body shook with impotent fury at the cool note of confidence in his tone. "We'll see about that!" she snapped, pivoting on her heel to walk jerkily away from him. When she spun to face him again her features were composed, her eyes gleaming maliciously.

"You're all threat, Annette; you always have been." Trace lifted his lips in a pitying smile. "Hot air and no ammunition," he concluded softly.

"Oh, really?" Her laughter was not a pleasant sound in the quiet room. "How's this for ammunition? Round one: you are a bachelor. Round two: your work necessitates your being away from home quite frequently. Round three: your home is located in an isolated area. Round four, and probably the most lethal of all: Kathy's only companion while you're away is an aging Mexican woman with a limited command of the English language." She smiled smugly. "I happen to think that's quite effective ammunition."

"Against the fact that you voluntarily gave up custody to Kathy?" Trace smiled wryly. "And the added fact that you've failed to take advantage of your visitation rights and have not even been here on several occasions when I've brought her east?" He shook his head. "I'd say your ammunition is about as effective as a pea-shooter against a mountain lion."

"We'll see, won't we?" Annette was now shaking with anger. "We'll see what *effect* my suit has after my witnesses, very well known and respected Philadelphians, have testified to my distraught, anguished state." Annette strolled arrogantly to him, sneering down at his sprawled form. "And after I testify how confused, rejected and unhappy I was feeling after Kathy's birth."

A tightness invading his chest, Trace slowly straightened in the chair. "All right, Annette, what do you want?" Even though he refused to let it show, asking the question cost him dearly in pride.

"Want?" Annette laughed in his face. "I'll tell you what I want. I want to make you suffer."

"Why, for God's sake?" Trace sprang to his feet, forcing Annette to retreat. "You accomplished that while we were married! It's been four damned years! You don't want Kathy, you never did. You know it as well as I. So why are you doing this? Why claim you want her now?"

As if she knew what his reaction would be, Annette backed farther away from him. "Because I know you *do* want her. And I know what it will do to you to lose her."

"But why should you care?" Frustration thickened his voice.

"Because I could never reach you, never touch you!" she shouted. "You were so damned self-contained inside your hotshot surgeon image. You gave me nothing!"

"Nothing?" Trace was so angry he had to whisper to keep from exploding. "Nothing? I gave you my love, my trust and my honor. What the hell else did you want?"

"My rightful place in society as the wife of San Antonio's leading neurosurgeon, that's what I wanted!" Annette was now trembling with fury. "*Your* love, *your* trust, *your* honor—" she spat the words at him "—I didn't want any of those any more than I wanted *you* or *your* brat!"

"You bitch!" Trace actually took a step toward her before he caught himself up short. "You position-hungry bitch!"

"Why don't you strike me?" Annette's eyes glittered with anticipation. "I wish you would. It would give me more evidence of exactly how unfit you are to have custody of a child!"

"I wouldn't waste the effort." Swinging away, Trace strode to the doorway where he paused to level a narrow-eyed glare at her. "You are not getting Kathy away from me, lawsuit or not."

Annette suddenly had a wild, frantic look. "I will get her! I must! Randall wants her!" As her own screamed words hit her, she clamped one fragile-looking hand over her mouth.

"Randall?" Trace repeated the name softly. "Randall who?" he began walking slowly toward her.

"Get out of here!" Annette shook her head wildly. "Get out of here before I call the police and have you thrown out!"

"Call them!" With a wave of one hand, Trace indicated the gold filigree French-style phone on the end table. "But, I give you my word you'll answer me before they can get here. Now, who the hell is this Randall?" Walking to within an inch of her, he glared directly into her frightened eyes. "And what does he want with *my* daughter?"

"I—I—"

His control breaking, Trace grasped her by the arms and shook her. "Answer me, damn you!"

"I'm going to marry him!" Annette blurted out jerkily.

"He has my condolences," Trace snarled. "What does that have to do with Kath?"

"Ran...Randall cannot father a child. He needs an heir." Annette cringed away from the expression on Trace's face.

"He can't have mine." Trace said each word distinctly. Dropping his hands as if touching her sickened him, Trace wheeled away from her. His hand was on the doorknob when Annette's voice stopped him.

"Randall can give me everything I ever wanted!" Her tone was strident. "He's very wealthy and prominent, and has an established place in Philadelphia society." Her eyes glittered with fervor. "I refuse to let you interfere with my plans. By the time my suit goes before a judge I will be Randall's wife." Her lip curled. "Which one of us do you think the judge will award Kathy to?"

Not bothering to reply, Trace pulled the door open. Annette's laughter followed him to the car.

His mind seething with impotent rage, Trace slammed the rental car into gear and tore away from the townhouse. Emotions churning, he handled the car recklessly on the narrow streets in the quaint restored section. Too stirred up to go back to the hotel he was staying in, he drove aimlessly for several minutes, searching his mind desperately for a way to thwart Annette.

Damn her! Cursing his former wife silently, Trace eyed a bar on the corner when he was forced to stop for a red light. He wanted a drink. No, what he really wanted was to hit something or someone! But he'd settle for a drink. As the light flicked to green he sent his gaze skimming the street for a vacant parking space and cursed again when he found none.

Positive that if he returned to his hotel room he'd pace the floor for the rest of the night, he slowed the car to a crawl, looking for a watering hole and human companionship.

Kate!

Even as her name popped into his mind Trace had a vision of her as she'd appeared earlier that day, her eyes smoky and her body taut with anger as she championed Kathy.

Without pausing to consider, Trace turned the car in the direction that would take him to the suburban community where he'd dropped Kate at her apartment building less than two hours before.

Dressed for bed in a very sheer, slip-style nightgown and a robe that had seen better days, Kate sat staring sightlessly at the TV screen while replaying the events of the preceding ten hours in her mind.

Well, one certainly couldn't say her Saturday had been dull, she thought wryly, stretching her arms over her head to flex tired muscles. There wasn't one thing dull about either one of the two people she'd spent the majority of her day with. And the smallest of the pair was an absolute doll!

A soft smile curving her lips, Kate drew her feet up under her robe and rested her head against the back of the sofa. Of all the children she'd ever met, Kate decided she liked Kathy the best. She'd never run across a child who was quite so impish and charming at the same time.

A low chuckle whispered through Kate's lips as she recalled Kathy's methods of soft-soaping her father—or attempting to!

Kathy's father—Kate's chuckled trailed away to a sigh—now there was a different story altogether. Trace Sinclair. What was one to make of a Trace Sinclair?

Impressions, some shadowy and unclear, others sharply defined, drifted in and out of her mind. Hard—gentle, impatient—forebearing, self-assured—hesitant. Electric! Exciting! Sexy!

Kate shivered. Trace was very much a man, and she was not immune to his masculine attraction. Strange, she had been seeing David for over six months, yet never in all that time had she felt the sensual fascination she'd experienced after only a few minutes in Trace's company.

Kate's bare toes curled at the memory of the alluring spell he cast. And he had more or less promised to kiss her before the evening was over—but he had not kept his promise.

After dinner, Trace had driven her directly home, bidding her a polite "good night" while she'd hugged and kissed Kathy. Now, over two hours later, Kate was amazed at the depth of disappointment she was still feeling because of his failure to keep his promise.

"Silly girl!"

Chiding herself, Kate slid off the sofa to flip through the TV channels in search of a good, late-night movie. What a way to spend a Saturday night, she thought wistfully, frowning at the flickering screen. Thanksgiving Day weekend and I'm faced with watching Cary Cooper ride off into the sunset!

Feeling restless and moody, and not even certain why, Kate turned the television off just as the doorbell rang.

David! Oh, no! Kate glanced at the digital clock on the TV, then at the door as the chime sounded for a second time. She didn't want to see David tonight; she didn't want to talk to him. As if the visitor was growing impatient, the ring peeled again, shrill, imperative. Sighing softly, she crossed the small room to the door, leaning forward to peek through the tiny hole.

The taut figure standing in the hallway was definitely not David Kendall. His shoulders hunched inside the suede jacket, his hands jammed into the deep pockets, Trace looked cold, impatient and more than a little angry.

Her breath suddenly erratic, Kate fumbled with the night chain and deadlock. Conscious of her appearance, she opened the door a few inches and peered around the edge of it.

"Trace, what are you..."

"May I come in, Kate?" Trace cut her off tersely.

"Trace, I'm not dressed!" Kate felt her cheeks flush. "I mean, I'm dressed for bed."

"Sounds good to me," he muttered. Slipping a hand from his pocket, he pushed gently against the door. "I came to talk, Kate, not to take you bar-hopping."

As he applied pressure to the door, Kate had little option but to let him in. Drawing her robe around her tightly, she retreated back to the sofa as Trace quietly closed and locked the door. The sound of the chain rattling into place caused a tingle along the length of her spine.

"Ah..." Kate had to pause to clear her throat. "What did you want to talk about?" she finally managed, watching him warily as he took off his jacket.

"The cold weather here in the east, the high cost of nearly everything—" Trace smiled slowly "—the fact that we both realize we want each other."

Kate's heartbeat seemed to come to a shuddering halt while a lump grew in her throat, making breathing difficult—if not completely impossible. Her mouth open in shock, she could do no more than stare at him for long seconds. During those seconds Trace moved to stand in front of her, his gaze steady on hers.

"I...ah...mmm...Trace, I, really...I..."

"Don't panic, Kate." Shaking his head at her feeble attempt at speech, he reached out to glide the tips of his fingers across her now flaming cheek. His smile grew decidedly sensuous at her shivery response. "I'm not going to force any issues here," he murmured.

Kate's breathing resumed as he removed his fingers and settled himself on the cushion beside her. Nervously smoothing her palm over the worn material of her robe, she studied his profile out of the corner of her eye.

"Well?"

"What?" Kate had become so engrossed in the unrelenting male beauty of his features that the sound of his voice startled her.

"I merely said 'well?'" Though his face remained impassive, his eyes gleamed with amusement. "You've practically dissected me with your eyes." Trace allowed his amusement to lift his lips in a smile. "Have you made a diagnosis?"

Embarrassed, Kate sniffed disdainfully. "I'm positive you're fully aware of how attractive you are." With an ease she was far from feeling, she turned to face him.

"Yes, I'm aware." His tone conveyed self-knowledge, not conceit. "The question is," Trace arched one brow rakishly. "Am I attractive to *you*?" Before she could begin to form an answer, he added, "As attractive as you are to me?"

Flustered by his directness, Kate lowered her eyes. "Trace, we've only just met!" she protested softly.

"Which means absolutely nothing, and you know it."
Though his tone was low, it held firm conviction. "There
is that indefinable 'something' flowing between us. It's
been there from the first moment our eyes met." Leaning toward her, he brushed his parted lips very lightly
over her cheek. Kate couldn't suppress the gasp of pleasure that burst from her lips. "You see what I mean?" Her
gasp became a moan when he teased the corner of her
mouth with the tip of his tongue. "Ah, Kate," he whispered enticingly, "I want to kiss you so badly my entire
body aches."

Her breath coming in shallow little spurts, Kate closed
her eyes. What should she do? What could she do? He
was too close. The musky male scent of him aroused
everything female in Kate. Her senses greedily drank in
the essence of him as she moved the fraction of an inch
necessary to slide her lips under his.

In the quiet room, Kate heard his breath hiss as he
drew it in sharply. For an instant his lips lay against hers
in breathless stillness. Then, with a sweet tenderness, his
mouth moved, slowly molding her lips to his. Surprisingly, there was no demand in the kiss, no urgency.
Gently, as if he was holding a fragile flower, he explored
the taste and texture of her lips.

Sighing softly, Kate leaned into the kiss, her body beginning to tremble as her breasts touched the hard plain
of his chest. She heard him groan, then the wonder of his
mouth was withdrawn.

"You're very new at this—aren't you?" His warm
breath caressed her lips. Kate shivered. "Have you ever
been with a man, Kate?"

"No." Raising strangely heavy eyelids, Kate stared up
at Trace in bemusement. "At least not in the way I think
you mean."

"I mean exactly what you think I mean." The tiny lines radiating from the corners of his eyes deepened, and Kate knew he was smiling at her. "You've never made love before?"

Kate shook her head mutely.

Trace expelled his breath very slowly. "I want to love you, Kate. You know that, don't you?" He drew his head back just far enough to gaze down at her. His eyes darkened as he watched her moisten her dry lips with her tongue.

"Trace, I..."

"You're afraid?" He murmured gently.

"Yes." Kate closed her eyes.

"Yet I can feel how you respond to me." One hand moved to capture her breast, fingers testing the hard readiness of the nipple. "Why are afraid?"

"When I opened the door for you, you looked so angry and—" she shrugged "—and so frustrated." Her lip caught between her teeth, Kate opened her eyes to stare up at him in mute appeal.

With a heaving sigh, Trace moved away from her to rest his head on the back of the sofa. "I was." Rolling his head to gaze at her, he smiled derisively. "Very angry and very frustrated," he admitted with dry self-mockery.

"Why?" Kate asked bluntly. "Were you angry at me?"

"No," Trace laughed softly. "But, I suppose I must have thought you might be the cure for both the emotional upsets."

Of course, Kate was consumed with curiosity. Wanting to know, yet hesitant to ask, she gazed at him indecisively. Trace gazed back, a tiny smile curving his lips—lips that Kate ached to feel pressed to hers again.

Certain he could read the longing in her eyes, she glanced down at her hands.

"What upset you, Trace?" Surprised at her own temerity, Kate kept her eyes averted. She could feel Trace stiffen and was on the verge of recinding her question when he sighed deeply.

"I had an argument with Annette," he said tersely.

Annette? Kate frowned—as much from the sudden dart of jealousy she felt as the confusion the name caused. Who was Annette? Lifting her head, she managed a cool stare.

"Annette?" Kate felt rather proud of her detached tone.

"Kathy's mother." Trace smiled grimly. "My ex-wife. She's been living with her parents since the divorce." His smile faded. "She was waiting for me when I took Kath back."

"And the argument made you angry," Kate concluded softly.

"No, the argument made me furious." Trace bit off a curse with a sharp shake of his head. "She's going to try to take Kath away from me." His lips twisted in a way that sent a shaft of fear through Kate. At the same time his eyes grew dark with pain so intense, Kate's heart ached for him.

"Oh, Trace, no!" Remembering Kathy's own words about her mother, Kate was powerless against the protest that rushed from her lips. "Kathy is so obviously happy with you!"

The flicker of understanding that moved across his face registered her concern. "I said she was going to *try*, Kate." His voice lowered dangerously. "I have no intention of letting her win...and I don't give a damn what I have to do to stop her."

At that moment, violence, terrifying in its intensity, seemed to flow from him, crackling the very air around him. Thankful she was not the one responsible for all that enmity, Kate shrank back into the corner of the sofa, actually feeling sympathy for his former wife. Her movement did not go undetected.

"I'm sorry, Kate." Raising his hand, Trace brushed the back of his fingers over her cheek. "I didn't really come here to dump my problems on you."

His hand still stroking her face, Trace shifted to lean over her. His lips hovered tantalizingly close to hers. Caught off guard by the lightning change in him, Kate gazed uncertainly into his eyes.

"In all honesty," he whispered, "I came here for very different reasons." Now the force field crackling around him was sensuous in origin and twice as potent. Turning his hand, he cradled her face in his palm. "I've been wanting to make love to you since lunchtime."

"But we only met at lunchtime!" Kate croaked, shuddering as his tongue moistened her dry lips.

"I know." His gliding tongue slid between her lips to trace the ridge of her teeth. "Strange, it seems I've been wanting you forever."

How she'd have responded to his observation, Kate was never to know, for with the last word, Trace crushed her mouth with his. This time there wasn't a hint of tenderness in his kiss. His lips were hard and urgent, demanding full participation from hers.

Thrilling to the sensations coursing through her body, Kate curled her arms around his tensely corded neck and kissed him back hungrily. Within seconds she was lost to reason and all sense of self-preservation.

Blindly, eagerly following his murmured urgings, Kate stretched out fully on the sofa, clinging to him as he moved to lay beside her. His chest crushed her breasts between them as his mouth sought hers. Drawing her lower lip between his own, Trace taught Kate things she'd never even imagined about kissing.

Kate was so warm, so very warm, yet shivering from the riot of sensations, which awoke desires that she'd thought existed only in imagination. Her breathing reduced to shallow little gasps, she speared her fingers through the silken strands of his hair and pressed her fingertips against him, urging him closer.

Drowning in a molten sea of hot pleasure, Kate was barely aware of Trace opening her robe. When his long hand enveloped her breast she moaned softly and arched her back. Accepting her silent invitation, Trace swiftly slid the robe from her. His gaze burning into her skin, he followed the motion as his hand slowly glided the narrow shoulder strap of her gown off her shoulder and down her arm, baring one full, taut breast.

"You're so very beautiful." Raising his eyes, Trace observed every nuance of expression on her face as his long fingers stroked her silken skin. "Haven't you ever been caressed like this before?" he murmured hoarsely.

Her head thrown back, lips parted, Kate could barely breathe, let alone speak. Moaning softly deep in her throat, she shook her head. Her silent denial was the truth. Never had she allowed a man to touch her like this.

"Has a man ever kissed you here?" Trace touched the aching tip with his finger.

Trembling in reaction, Kate again shook her head. Her breath escaping as mere puffs, she watched as Trace, a satisfied smile curing his mouth, lowered his head to her breast. An exquisite pain uncurled in her body when his lips closed over her aroused nipple.

"Oh!...oh, God, Trace!" The cry burst from Kate's tight throat at the flicking touches of his tongue. She heard herself whimper when he gently began suckling.

Kate was no longer warm; she was burning. A rush of feelings, wild, crazy, swept her away. Murmuring little, incoherent sounds in her throat, she arched into his hungry mouth, her body undulating sensuously against him. A soft protest whispered through her lips when he withdrew from her breast only to become a sigh of delight when Trace fastened his mouth to hers.

Passion building, Trace coaxed her lips apart, then plunged his tongue deeply into the honeyed sweetness of her mouth. With a low, growllike rumble, he plundered her mouth in an evocative rhythm.

Restless with the tension coiling in her body, Kate skimmed her hands down his back, kneading his taut muscles with the tips of her fingers, scoring his shirt with her nails.

"Yes," he urged raggedly, sliding his lips from her mouth to the curve of her neck. "Touch me, Kate. Love me with your hands." Drawing back, Trace practically tore the shirt from his body. "Please, touch me, Kate!" His tongue etched erotic designs on the sensitive skin at the curve of her neck. His hair-roughened chest brushed tantalizingly over the tips of her breasts.

Kate needed no further urging. Loving the feel of his heated skin against her palms, she stroked and caressed his back and chest. Her own excitement went spiraling out of control at his sharply indrawn breath when her nails scraped his flat male nipples.

Sweet, hot desire flowed through her. Kate parted her legs when his hand stroked the quivering flesh of her inner thigh, and she arched into his touch as his palm cupped the heart of her desire.

"Kate. Kate. Kate." A whisper. Her name. Nothing more. Yet, inside her head, the need contained within those whispered words became a shouted plea.

Reacting instinctively, Kate moved to accommodate him as Trace slid his body between her thighs. Even through his clothes the extent of his arousal was evident. When Trace thrust his hips into hers, Kate gasped with surprise and shock.

Four

What was she doing? The intrusive thought pierced the fog of passion clouding Kate's mind and cooled the heated response of her restless body.

She did not know this man! Why was she reacting to him with such intensity? Did she really want to offer him the gift of herself? Kate shivered from the force of her doubts.

The shiver turned into a shudder of exquisitely renewed pleasure as Trace again sought her breasts.

Helplessly obeying the urges controlling her body, Kate moved sensuously beneath him. She wanted Trace badly, ached for the fulfillment he could give her, and even as her mind argued for a cautious withdrawal, she could not deny the craving she felt for him.

Sensing her conflict, Trace lifted his head to gaze at her soberly.

"What is it, Kate?" The strain in his voice was a barometer, indicating the control he was exerting over his own clamoring body. "You're only with me halfway now. What's going on inside your head?"

Kate moved her head distractedly on the sofa cushion. "I...Trace, I...don't know but, I'm..."

"'Scared?" Trace finished for her, his lips curving in a surprisingly understanding smile.

"Yes." Embarrassed by the intensity of her unbridled behavior, Kate lowered her lashes to conceal the gleam of tears in her eyes.

"There's no reason to be, you know." Sighing, Trace moved to lay beside her, still touching, but less intimately.

Kate opened her eyes in time to see Trace close his. Her lip caught between her teeth, she watched as his chest heaved in deep, controlled breaths.

"God, I want you, Kate!" he muttered hoarsely, opening his eyes to stare into hers. "I want you so very much." His lips twisted derisively. "But not so much that I'd take you like this." His smile gentled as he tapped her temple with his forefinger. "I want you willing and eager for me...in your mind as well as your body."

Heat suffused Kate's face as Trace carefully slid her nightgown into place. Feeling utterly stupid, she stammered into an apology. "Oh, Trace, I—I'm sorry!" Raising her hand she stroked his beard-stubbled cheek. "I want you too. I really do! But..." her voice trailed away to nothingness.

"But you're not quite ready," Trace again completed her faltering explanation. "I know." Lifting his hand he captured hers, holding it against his face. "You're very young, my lovely Kate. So very young," he murmured sadly.

"I'll be twenty-four on Christmas Day!" Kate protested. "That's not *very* young!"

"In comparison to my thirty-five it is." Settling more comfortably beside her, he propped his head on his hand and gazed down at her, a teasing smile playing at the corners of his mouth. "I've got eleven years and eons of experience on you, kid."

"But I'm a fast learner!" Kate blurted rashly. "Don't give up on me, Trace!"

"Oh, Kate, you're priceless!" His laughter began as a low rumble in his chest, then exploded into a roar, warming Kate as it swirled around her. "Come to Texas with me, Kate." Trace's half-joking plea tugged at her heart.

"You know that's impossible, Trace," she chided softly.

"Nothing's impossible, innocent one." His smile crooked, Trace rubbed his nose against hers. "If you won't come to Texas, come to breakfast with me tomorrow morning, and stay for dinner." His teeth nipped playfully on her lower lip. "And maybe even longer," he whispered enticingly.

"I did have a previous engagement." Kate was suddenly finding it difficult to breathe again. Holding her breath she endured the mind-scattering sensation of his tongue stroking the spot he'd moments ago caught between his teeth. "I'll..." Kate gulped. "I'll break the date!" His tongue darted teasingly into her mouth. "Oh, God, Trace! What time do you want me?"

"A very inviting question," Trace murmured against her lips, soft laughter evident in his voice. "I ache to give the obvious answer...but I'll contain myself."

"You're laughing at me." Try as she might, Kate could not prevent the hurt from tingeing her tone.

"No, darling, I'm laughing at myself." Giving her a final, hard kiss, Trace swung his legs to the floor and stood up. "I'm going to get out of here before I laugh myself into trouble." A tender smile tilting his lips, he held his hand out to help her up. "Do you trust me enough to come to my hotel for breakfast?"

"In your room?" Kate paused in the act of pulling on her robe to blink at him.

Shaking his head at her, he chuckled again. "No, funny Kate, in the hotel coffee shop." His gleaming eyes held both question and challenge. "I'm staying at the Hershey. Will you come?"

"Yes." Noting his satisfied smile, Kate followed him to the door. It was not until she'd agreed to meet him in the coffee shop at ten, and he'd stepped into the hallway that she added, "I'd have come to your room, Trace." When he arched his brows mockingly, she said softly, "I trust you that much already."

"Thank you, Kate." Leaning toward her he brushed his mouth over hers, then turned away abruptly. "See you at ten," he called as he rounded the corner at the end of the short hall.

A smile of bemusement on her soft lips, Kate closed and locked the door. Absently switching off the lights, she drifted into her bedroom. A glow of warm anticipation tingling through her, she tossed her robe onto the foot of the bed, then slid between the covers.

What was one to make of a Trace Sinclair? Kate asked herself dreamily, forgetting to switch off the bedside light as she sank into a reverie of the time they'd spent together.

Trace was almost back to his hotel in the city when he realized that for the past few hours he'd completely forgotten Annette and her threat.

Reflectively, his grip tightened on the steering wheel. Damn her! The only way she'll get Kath from me is over my dead body. The silent vow still rang in his mind when memory sent a smile to his grimly set lips.

"The only way you'll take a belt to this child is over my dead body!"

Trace could still hear the outrage that had quivered in Kate's voice when she'd thrown the challenge at him. His smile grew wider, then he frowned as pain registered on his conscience. Glancing down at his hands, he was amazed to see his knuckles were white.

Trace cursed his former wife as he loosened his death grip on the steering wheel. There had to be a way to stop her from getting custody of Kath. A way that would not mean depriving Kathy of the genuine love of her maternal grandparents.

Anger again began churning through his body. Trace turned the rented car over to the hotel's valet parking attendant and went to his room only to pace the floor in restless frustration.

How had he ever convinced himself that Annette would be the perfect lifetime partner for him? Shaking his head in disgust, Trace flung his body into a chair. How many times had he asked himself that same question since Annette had revealed her true colors?

God! Were all females scheming and dishonest in their quests to attain their goals in life? When he'd first met Annette, seven years before, she'd appeared the most gentle, understanding woman he'd ever run across.

The memory of that meeting and the subsequent ugliness of their marriage twisted Trace's lips as though with a bitter taste.

At twenty-eight Trace was already being praised throughout San Antonio for his skill in the operating room. His hands and mind were sure and incisive, his methods innovative. He was well on the way to carving a name for himself in medical circles throughout the country.

His success had not come without cost. Long hours of work and short respites for rest had left Trace numb to the ego trip that usually accompanies sudden adoration. Trace was simply too weary to be impressed—either with himself or anyone else.

That is until the afternoon he was introduced to the house guest of a colleague of his. The occasion was a barbecue at the home of the head of neurosurgery.

Trace had not wanted to attend the affair; even when he had no surgery scheduled he had time-consuming paperwork to do. The chief neurosurgeon had not extended an invitation, he'd issued an order: "You'd better be there." Trace went, muttering imprecations all the way.

From the moment Trace sauntered onto the patio of his chief's home, he saw little but the exquisitely lovely young woman seated with his colleague's wife. The woman was small, dainty, and the most beautiful woman he'd seen in years. There was a soft, gentle look about her that drew him like a homing device.

As he approached the two women, Bette, his colleague's wife, smiled widely.

"Oh, here's our glory-boy now!" Laughing at his frown of disapproval, she extended one plump hand to him. "Trace, come meet a friend from my college days."

Her name was Annette Parker, and her voice was as beautiful as the rest of her. Within half an hour of their polite greetings, Trace had learned that Annette was from a moderately well-off, Philadelphia family; that she had graduated from University of Pennsylvania; that she belonged to the Junior League and did volunteer work; and as she had no burning desire for a career, worked part-time for the firm which employed her father as a vice-president.

Soft, bitter laughter shattered the silence of the dimly lit room. Resting his head against the back of the chair, Trace reflected on how perfectly clear hindsight was. Now, seven years removed from their first meeting, he sardonically applauded Annette's consummate act of assumed gentleness. Of course, now Trace knew too well that Annette was as gentle as a black widow spider—the only difference being, she didn't want to devour him, merely his social position in the community. And it had taken less than three years for her to reveal her true colors.

Growling a curse of disgust, both for himself and Annette, Trace surged to his feet to pace the impersonal room, one hand agitatedly raking through his hair.

What an utter fool he'd made of himself over her! Though unpalatable, Trace faced the truth squarely. True, he'd nearly worked himself to the point of exhaustion in the months preceding her advent into his life and had very probably been ripe for picking by cleverly directed feminine fingers. But that in no way excused his behavior, or his tolerance of hers. He'd behaved like a love-sick teenager in the throes of first passion.

Made uncomfortable by his reflections, Trace prowled the room, finally coming to a stop at the window that overlooked the broad center city street.

Trace didn't want to look back, didn't want to remember, yet the fury coursing through his veins would not allow relaxation. In an effort to purge his system of Annette's poison, he deliberately unlocked the door he'd slammed on memory four years before.

Playing her role to the hilt, Annette had insisted on a very proper courtship, even after she'd returned to her home two weeks from the day Trace met her. Since she'd aroused him unbearably, yet left him frustrated, he'd continued his pursuit long distance via phone calls, and flowers with little notes, and long, impassioned letters.

When, after four lonely, fantasy-filled months, she agreed to marry him, Trace had practically worked himself to a standstill. Tired but triumphant, he journeyed east to meet his future in-laws, Ruth and William Parker. Expecting to spend a few days in Philadelphia before whisking Annette back to Texas with him, Trace had his hopes dashed again when she informed him she wanted to have a large wedding at home.

Beginning to feel desperate, Trace agreed to all her demands and went back to Texas alone. Annette kept him abreast of the ongoing, elaborate wedding plans by lengthy, long-distance calls.

There were times during the intervening months when Trace felt on the verge of climbing the walls. He hadn't been with a woman since weeks before meeting Annette, and he wanted her so badly that merely thinking about her gave him the shakes.

Then, finally, the day came for him to fly east. After what seemed like an endless round of parties for the couple, Trace at last stood in the old, stately church the

Parkers attended and watched in bemusement as his bride slowly walked down the aisle to him, his heart swelling with the pride of realization that the beautiful woman was his.

Following a lavish, endless wedding reception, Trace escaped to Hawaii for two weeks of bliss with his bride.

Harsh laughter bounced off the cold windowpane—a raspy sound from a tight throat. Well, Trace thought wryly, his plan had been for two weeks of bliss when he'd made the reservations for their honeymoon. From the way Annette had responded to him before the wedding, he'd every reason to expect an ardent bride in his bed. Her frigid attitude soon put a damper on his expectations. Though not completely cold, her response could only be described as lukewarm at the best of times. And then only after he'd debased himself by begging.

"Oh hell!"

Swinging away from the window, Trace began pacing again. Why *had* he allowed the memories to surface after all these years? He didn't want to remember the times he'd swallowed his pride to coax and cajole that unresponsive, cold-hearted witch! God! Why, how had he continued to love her?

Because out of the bedroom she was so charming, that's why, Trace jeered. At least, he qualified, Annette was charming until he cut her ration of social functions. And that was when she'd revealed her true self. Up until that point, though hating it, Trace had squired Annette to as many functions as he could manage with the schedule he maintained. It was at these affairs that Annette was at her most shining, charming best.

Always a loner, Trace had shunned the many social gatherings he was invariably invited to. His rare, free hours were precious, and he preferred to spend them quietly. While waiting to claim his bride, he'd eagerly looked forward to spending those quiet moments with her. On their return to San Antonio, Annette had quickly changed that idea. She made no bones about demanding the glittering social whirl his position entitled her to.

Disillusioned, but still wildly infatuated with her, Trace had indulged her for almost two years. He even rented an apartment in the city, conveniently near both his office and the hospital. Then one night while dressing to go out to yet another of the endless affairs, tired beyond belief and sick with self-disgust, Trace had stopped dead in the process of buttoning his elegantly pleated shirt to stare at Annette with eyes that had lost the glow of adoration.

"The hell with this," he said tersely, shrugging out of the shirt. "I'm beat, and I'm not going anywhere. You may go alone if you wish."

Exquisitely gowned in a Paris original, Annette had merely gaped at him in shock for several minutes. Then she gave her best performance to date. First she tried anger. Then she tried tears. And then, when the realization dawned that it wasn't moving Trace, she tried sex.

Perhaps it was understandable that Trace's firmness wavered, then crumbled; he'd waited so long, wanted so badly.

The very sad thing was that, even before the loving was over, Trace felt nothing but crushing disappointment. And, more sadly still, he was forced to admit to himself that he no longer cared.

But the final, irrevocable blow fell when Annette first suspected that she was pregnant a few weeks later.

Up at his usual early hour, Trace had surprised her in the bathroom, being violently sick. Moved by compassion, he'd supported her until the shudders had subsided. When he stepped back she turned on him, her eyes frantic, her lips twisted with fury.

"Damn you!" she'd shouted. "Damn you for getting difficult at the exact time I had to stop taking the pill! Now look what's happened!"

Stunned, Trace had stared at her blankly, his mind digesting her accusation with incredulity. He was a doctor—and he hadn't even known his wife was taking birth control pills!

"Is it so terrible?" he finally asked. "We've been married for two years, Annette." Trace smiled tenderly—after all, she was very likely a little scared…and *he* was going to be a father! "It's not too soon to start a family."

"Never is too soon!" Annette cried shrilly. "I have just established myself in the best San Antonion circles! I'll lose ground—I can't be pregnant now!" She raised one delicate hand imploringly. "Trace, you're a doctor. You can do something, you've *got* to do something!"

A chill pervading his body, Trace said carefully, "What, exactly, do you want me to do?" He knew the answer she'd give; he could feel it in his bones. Yet, when it came, it wrenched his heart just the same.

"Get rid of it!" Annette wailed. "Admit me to the hospital and take it out. I can't bear the thought of it!"

It was dead. The love, or infatuation, or whatever it was that Trace had felt for her was suddenly completely dead; Annette had killed it with her whining plea.

"No, Annette, I won't do that," Trace said with a steadiness he fought to maintain. "Nor will I allow any other physician in this city to do it. The child is mine, and I want it."

"Well, I don't!" Annette screamed. "I don't want either you or your brat! Do you understand that?"

A low growling noise broke the silence of the night. Standing rigid in the middle of the Philadelphia hotel room, Trace shrugged, as if freeing himself of a burden. As if he'd forgotten where he was he glanced around the room. A wry smile touched his tight lips when his gaze settled on the bed.

Trace had walked out of the bedroom the morning Annette had screamed that she did not want him or his "brat." He had not shared a bed with her or any other woman since then. His celibacy was self-imposed. Trace was determined that never again would he be vulnerable to any woman.

With a bright smile and a cheery "hello" to the doorman, Kate breezed through the wide hotel doors at two minutes to ten the following morning. Her lustrous black hair bouncing on her shoulders in time with her jaunty step and her gray eyes gleaming with good health, she looked thoroughly relaxed and carefree. Her appearance was a facade; inside her stomach, a million nerve-endings she hadn't realized she owned were busy tying themselves into hard little knots.

How would Trace behave with her this morning, she wondered nervously, crossing the spacious lobby to the coffee shop. Would he be warm or cool, friendly or distant…would he show up?

The questions which had tormented her from the moment she woke up were answered as she entered the coffee shop. Trace was already there and, as if he'd been watching the doorway for her, he got to his feet and pulled the chair next to his out for her, a dazzling smile of welcome enhancing his attractive face.

"Good morning, Kate," he murmured as she slid onto the chair. "From the color on your nose and cheeks, I'd hazzard a guess that it's cold outside."

Smiling her thanks as he slipped her jacket from her shoulders, Kate nodded. "There's a brisk wind." Her nostrils flared as she inhaled the inviting aroma of freshly brewed coffee. "It bites at the exposed areas."

"So do I," Trace teased softly, settling himself close beside her. "And the covered areas too."

Embarrassed, but pleasantly so, Kate glanced around the half-filled room. Satisfied that there were no patrons within hearing distance, she brought her quelling gaze back to him, her head moving back and forth in despair.

"Trace, really! If anyone heard, they'd think—"

"But never in public places," his laughing voice overrode hers. "If anyone heard me they'd think—what?" Arched eyebrows demanded she finish what she'd started to say.

"That..." Kate looked directly into his eyes. "They'd think that we were lovers," she said softly.

"They'd be close to right." Trace shrugged his unconcern. "And, before too long, I fully intend making sure they *would* be right." His gaze noted the renewed color in her cheeks. Gliding his hand over hers, he entwined their fingers. "I want very badly to be your first lover, Kate," he said distinctly. Then, very softly, "And I think you want that too."

"Trace, I...I..." Flustered by his bluntness, Kate searched for a response—*any* response. She could hardly admit that his assertion was correct, and that she *did* want him to be her first lover. Lost for words, she shook her head distractedly.

"Don't go spinning off into space, smoke-eyes." Trace's eyes darkened to the shade of jade with amusement. "I did say I wouldn't make an issue of it." His lips curved appealingly. "In fact, I'm going to let you decide when and where." The smile faded as he grew serious, "Okay?"

"Yes." Kate gave him a trembly smile of relief. "And...thank you. You could easily have...ah, resolved the issue last night, you know?"

Trace smiled in understanding. "Yes, honey, I do know. But, thank *you* for being so honest with me." His smile curved wryly. "I find honesty in a woman rather refreshing."

A tingle of unease slid down Kate's spine; what *had* gone wrong with his marriage? More importantly—what was she getting herself into here? She had problems of her own; she wasn't sure she was up to handling bitterness and cynicism from him. And yet, unaccountably, she felt an overwhelming urge to reassure him.

"I will always be honest with you, Trace."

A subtle change altered his expression from wryness to appreciation of the somber steadiness of her tone. "And I promise I will always be honest with you, Kate," he returned her vow quietly.

As had happened over the dinner table the night before, Kate got lost in the beckoning lure of his cool green eyes. Unaware of the passage of time, or the bustle of activity as a large group of people entered the coffee shop, she stared into those cool depths, her lips parted slightly with the wonder of the longing tugging her toward him.

"I think we'd better order breakfast."

"What...?" Kate blinked, shook her head fractionally, then refocused on his austerely set face. Even as a flush of embarrassment warmed her throat, she realized that Trace had been affected by that strange, trancelike moment as well. The echo of his passion-roughened tone whispered through her mind, and his eyes were bright with heat from within. As the flush mounted to her cheeks, his lips tilted in a heart-stopping, tender smile.

"I said, I think we'd better order breakfast," Trace repeated softly, his smile growing into a teasing grin, "before we get thrown out of here for indecent exposure."

Indecent exposure? Kate's blankness lasted only an instant, then her face blossomed with understanding. Had she been that transparent? Had the yearning she was feeling for him blazed out of her eyes?

Of course it had. Catching her lower lip between her teeth, Kate found little comfort in the knowledge that Trace's eyes had revealed an equal measure of desire.

"Don't, honey." Strong fingers applied reassuring pressure to hers. "There's nothing to feel embarrassed about." Lifting her hand he brought it to his lips to bestow a warm, brief kiss. "The feeling is mutual." As Trace lowered her hand to the table, his eyes began dancing with devilry. "The hell with the rest of the world." Rakishly raised eyebrows invited her to join in with his devil-may-care attitude.

"Is that any way for a physician to talk?" Feeling suddenly free and feather-light, Kate grinned at him, shaking her gleaming hair back with an abandoned toss of her head.

Trace's soft laughter flowed over Kate like warm honey. "There you go again," he teased as his laughter subsided. "Exactly how is a physician supposed to talk?"

"In deep, confident tones," Kate shot back, reflecting his light mood. "In a manner befitting his serious occupation."

"No kidding! Befitting even?" Trace contrived to look amazed. "I never knew that. I'll have to practice—befitting, I mean."

Although they seemed to be laughing constantly, both Kate and Trace managed to consume an enormous breakfast, beginning with fruit cups and ending with blueberry blintzes.

"Good heavens!" Kate groaned, replacing her empty coffee cup on the saucer. "I don't think I'll be able even to think about food for at least a week!"

"I'll bet you the price of a movie ticket that you'll be moaning you're starving by dinner time." Trace issued the challenge with a grin.

"We're going to see a movie?" Kate asked hopefully.

Trace chuckled at her eagerness. "After dinner, if you like." He tilted his head questioningly, "Is it a bet?"

Positive she wouldn't want as much as one more bite of food for the remainder of the day, Kate smiled smugly. "You're on," she agreed, then qualified, "on one condition."

"Name it," Trace said expansively.

"I get to pick the film."

"You drive a hard bargain, woman," Trace frowned. "But, okay, you get to pick the film."

A twitch at the corners of his lips ruined the effect of his frown as he stood up and tossed an over-large tip on the table for the waitress. Then, after scooping the check up, he nudged Kate into movement with a gentle taunt.

"I think we've taken up space in here long enough." Tipping his head he drew her attention to the restless line of people waiting for tables. "Perhaps we'd better leave before we're asked to vacate the premises."

It was not until Kate was patiently standing beside Trace at the cash register that she noticed the rain-spattered look of some of the people waiting in line and the dripping umbrellas in the hands of others.

"Trace, it's raining outside," she murmured as they made their way around the line and strolled into the hotel lobby.

"So I see." Carrying her jacket over one arm, Trace curled the other arm around the back of her waist, gently propelling her to the wide windows that faced the street.

In communal silence they stood for several minutes, staring out at the rain, sheeting at an almost horizontal angle from the force of the wind. A shiver feathered Kate's shoulders and arms at the sight of the few pedestrians she watched, hurrying along, huddled beneath umbrellas buffeted by the wind.

Feeling the tremor that ran through her, Trace tightened his arm to draw her close to the warmth of his body.

"Not exactly inviting—is it?" He voiced her thoughts correctly.

"No," Kate sighed. "Had you planned anything for today?"

"I was going to suggest that you show me the sights," Trace shrugged. "But it's hardly the weather for sightseeing."

Seeing the prospects for a day spent in his company dwindling, Kate looked up at him dejectedly. "Would you prefer to take me home?"

"Home?" Trace repeated hollowly. "Do you want to go home?"

"Oh, no!" Kate cried, shaking her head. "But, what else can we do?"

A satisfied smile curled the edges of his lips. "We could go up to my room and play doctor," he suggested wickedly.

Five

Kate tried very hard to appear both shocked and affronted. But even with her teeth clamped together, the bubbling laughter his outrageous suggestion elicited burst through her lips.

"But Trace! There's not a thing wrong with either my head or back!" she gasped through her fit of giggles.

"Brat!" His low growl was muttered close to her ear as he bent over her shaking body. "Okay, let's go up to my room and talk." Tightening his hold on her waist, Trace turned them both in the direction of the elevators. Before striding out, he paused to glance down at her. "Okay?" Though his voice held firm, there was a shadow of uncertainty in his eyes which tugged at Kate's heart.

"Okay," she agreed softly. The tug in her chest curled happily as the uncertainty in his eyes was banished by a glimmer of undisguised pleasure.

Since the elevator held three other people, they rode up to his floor in silence. It was not until they were standing in front of the door to his room that Trace leveled a solemn look at her.

"You don't have to be at all nervous, you know," he said reassuringly. "I'm not going to ask anything from you that you are not prepared to give willingly."

Kate fully realized that she could be acting very foolishly; after all, she hardly knew the man! Yet, for reasons incomprehensible to her, she trusted him to the marrow of her bones. Foolish? Perhaps, but there it was.

"I'm not nervous, Trace." Kate's voice was soft with honest simplicity. A teasing smile lit her face. "Had I been nervous, I'd have bolted for safety when you made the suggestion."

For an instant, Trace stared at her as if held in breathless stillness. Then, a devastatingly beautiful smile transformed his face and he flung his arm around her shoulders, hugging her close to him.

"You know," he observed softly as he inserted the door key and pushed the door open. "Every overworked doctor should have at least one Kate in his life." His arm still clamping her to his side, Trace shepherded Kate into the room, releasing her as he turned to shut the door quietly behind them.

Deeply affected by the meaning contained within the deceptively casual compliment, and not quite sure how to respond, Kate walked slowly to the wide window. A glowing warmth seeping through her, she stared sightlessly at the rain-washed pane, her mind revolving with the echo of the words: *In his life. In his life.*

"Kate?"

The confusion in Trace's low voice drew Kate away from her bemusement over an emotion too tenuous to name. Blinking her eyes as if emerging from a trance, she slowly turned to face him.

"Hmm?" Kate was unaware of the dreamy, faraway sound of her voice.

"Is there something wrong?" Eyes narrowed, Trace scrutinized her expression.

"Wrong?" Kate frowned. "No, of course not." She waved her hand as if waving aside the very idea. "Why do you ask?"

Trace tilted his head, one eyebrow arching quizzically. "Why? I asked because you suddenly seemed to withdraw into yourself." His lips curved ruefully. "Are you having second thoughts about being alone with me?"

"Not at all!" Kate denied at once. "If I seemed to withdraw it was just..." she smiled self-consciously. "To tell the truth, I was just very flattered by what you said."

"About every busy doctor needing a Kate!" he exclaimed. "Honey, if that's your idea of thought provoking flattery, you've been hanging out with the wrong guys!"

"Trace Sinclair! I have not been *hanging* out with any guys!" Kate protested laughingly.

Trace grinned. "Yeah, I know." Walking over to her he caught her hand to lead her to the settee beside the window. "I have...ah, proof of that." His grin widened. "You're so innocent it scares me."

On examination, Kate decided Trace didn't look at all scared. As a matter of fact, he looked as bold as brass and equal to anything—especially a twenty-three-year-old virgin. Curling into the corner of the settee, she drew her legs up under her and grinned back at him.

"Well, in that case," Kate drawled the curve, then fired the fast break, "maybe I can scare some answers out of you."

With his long legs stretched out, booted ankles crossed, head resting on the amply padded back of the settee, Trace had the appearance of a completely relaxed man. His easy smile reinforced the appearance.

"Maybe," he drawled lazily. "Why don't you give it a shot?"

Kate's hesitation lasted only long enough to marshal her questions into order.

"Okay, here goes. I know you're thirty-five, about six feet tall, and more attractive than is probably good for you...or any member of the opposite sex." Kate managed to keep a straight face when Trace laughed softly in appreciation of her description. But her lips trembled with a smile at his calm acceptance of her evaluation.

"Too true." His shrug was casually elegant; his eyes danced with amusement. "But I do love hearing it." He worked his features into an avid expression, "Please, do go on."

Kate lost the battle of control with her mirth. "You're retiring attitude underwhelms me!" she gasped. "I think you missed your calling. You should've gone into acting."

"Hey, yeah! I never thought of that." In all seriousness, Trace went along with her silliness. "Gee, not only would I have made a lot more money, I'd have all those delectable aspiring actresses crawling all over me." He produced a leering grin. "Damn! Where were you when I was making a career choice?" he demanded with mock gruffness.

"Very likely still in diapers," Kate retorted.

Trace grabbed his ribs as if he'd been injured. "Oh, cheap shot, kid!" he objected. "That barb caught me where I live—right on the ole ego."

Suddenly the laughter died on Kate's lips, and she gazed at him wistfully. "You think I'm too young for you, don't you?"

Trace became abruptly serious. "Aren't you?" he asked tautly.

Regretting her gibe, Kate stared into his eyes, which had taken on an emerald hue. "No," she answered very simply.

"The span involves more than mere numbers, Kate." Trace attempted a smile, failed, then gave up the effort. "It encompasses a great deal of painfully earned experience and maturity."

"I realize that, but..." Kate groped for words that would exactly define her position. "I may be inexperienced, Trace, but I do consider myself a mature adult." Her smile grew sadly reminiscent. "One tends to mature very quickly in a family of forever young advocates."

"That's a teaser, honey," Trace said quietly. "Let's have some clarification."

Kate was immediately sorry she'd offered the explanation. She wanted to learn about Trace, talk about him...not herself. She especially didn't want to elaborate on the whys and wherefores of herself. She started to shake her head in denial; Trace wouldn't accept the motion.

"Spill it, kid," he ordered gently.

And spill Kate did. Though she began slowly, hesitantly, the story poured out of her with increasing swiftness until she was empty, drained by the barrenness of the years she chronicled.

"I suppose my family would be classified as average—middle class. One husband. One wife. Two children. The obligitory first-born son, my brother Scott, and yours truly, the baby daugther. There is, of course, the required ranch-style house in a planned suburban community. Nothing posh, you understand, but acceptable."

As she was now looking inside herself, Kate was immune to the waiting stillness gripping Trace. It was at this point in her narrative that Kate's words began racing off her tongue.

"My parents arrived at this middle-class station via the mass transit of individually pursued careers. To maintain it, my mother continued on in her chosen field—with short absence leaves to give birth."

"A common enough practice in today's economy," Trace inserted carefully.

"Yes, unfortunately it is," Kate agreed cynically. "As is the running, faster and faster, merely to maintain the place or status." Her smile was devoid of humor as she explained. "You know, the constant jockeying for position." Her lips twisted into a grimace. "What's that?" Raven-wing eyebrows arched. "You say the neighbors two streets down had their patio flag-stoned? Well, it must be time to have the rec-room remodeled into a facsimile of a twenties speakeasy."

"It's called keeping up with the Jones'," Trace murmured.

Kate laughed bitterly. "I'll say, and then some. But completely harmless, unless children are neglected while the adults are playing their funny little games."

Trace frowned. "You were neglected?"

"Oh, not in the physical sense," Kate said hastily. "Scott and I were well cared for in that respect; well fed, well dressed...very well dressed. We were taken for medical and dental check-ups regularly." She smiled widely to reveal perfectly even, white teeth. "The orthodontist's bill was a dandy—and my teeth weren't even very crooked to begin with."

"Well then?" Trace moved uneasily—as if becoming uncomfortable with his thoughts.

"Emotional poverty," Kate said distinctly. "Too many hours spent in the company of uninterested nursery school employees and baby-sitters. Too many birthdays and holidays spent with all the 'right' people, who were not necessarily friends. Too many achievements ignored or overlooked because of a dinner party that absolutely couldn't be missed, or an opportunity to move up the social ladder that simply could not be passed up."

"Kate..." Trace began sympathetically.

"Do you have any idea what it's like to watch your parents flirting outrageously with near strangers?" she went on as if she hadn't heard him. "Can you imagine what it does to an impressionable teenager to observe her mother give the come-on to a man she barely knows simply because it's an accepted part of the game of staying-in-place?"

"No," Trace said quietly.

"Emotional poverty—in capital letters."

Trace's eyes narrowed thoughtfully. "And that's why you were so bristly at our first meeting," he mused softly. "You thought I'd 'mislaid' Kathy by sheer carelessness." When Kate averted her face, Trace caught her chin to make her look at him. "You believed I was caught up in the moves of those 'funny little games'—didn't you?"

"No," Kate admitted. "I thought you were even worse. I was sure you were completely careless of your daughter."

"Ah, Kate, protector of lost children," Trace murmured, the expression on his face heart-wrenchingly tender as he gazed down at her. "Is that your mission in life—looking out for emotionally poor kids?"

The hand gently cupping her face moved caressingly along her jaw line, long fingers stroking, testing the satiny texture of her cheek. Kate's skin tingled, sending shock waves all the way to her toes.

"N-not at all!" she exclaimed on a quickly drawn breath. "I...I..." Kate's voice faltered as the fingers slid sensuously down the length of her throat.

"You...you...what?" Trace murmured, exploring her collarbone with the tips of his fingers. "What do you want out of life, Kate?"

Kate trembled as his fingers drew a gliding pattern on her skin from her collarbone to the fluttering pulse at the base of her neck.

"I want to be a wife and a mother," Kate answered with all the honesty she'd promised him. "A *full*-time wife and mother." She smiled deprecatingly. "An ambition not at all in vogue, I know. But that's what I want out of life—eventually."

"Emotional security?" Trace queried softly, denying the urge to send his itching fingers to trace the edge of her blouse.

"Yes," Kate answered simply. "I don't know if I'll ever really attain it, but I know I must try."

"And is there a special man right now?" he asked casually. "One you think might be suitable to play the role of husband in your plans?" His eyes were coolly remote as he watched her with unnerving steadiness.

Trace was silently demanding Kate live up to her promise of honesty. She gave in to his demand without hesitation.

"No," she replied with equal steadiness, "there is no special man."

"You're not seeing *any*one?" Trace asked skeptically.

"I didn't say that," Kate corrected blandly. "I have been seeing a man the past few months but, I decided to end the relationship because he was getting too possessive." Her smile was sadly gentle. "He wasn't at all special, you see."

"Very clearly." Trace didn't smile, but his fingers moved with nerve-jarring slowness, gliding erratically along the edge of her blouse lapel. "You weren't at all tempted, hmm?" His fingers came to a stop at the first fastened button, an inch or so above the valley between her breasts.

There wasn't a chance he'd miss her responding quiver, and Kate knew it. Not even bothering to hide her reaction to his touch, she murmured, "Not even a little bit."

"And now?" Trace was no longer looking at her. His eyes darkening to dense forest green, he observed the pattern his fingers were tracing on her flesh. "Are you tempted now?"

Tempted? Had Kate been able to spare a shallow breath she might have laughed. As it was she could barely speak.

"You know I am."

A tiny, exciting smile lifted the corners of his lips. "May I open the button?" Trace flicked at the small pearlized stud with his index finger.

Kate paused for a breathless moment, during which her mind raced with conflicting emotions. Without a shred of doubt she knew that were she to ask him to stop he would do so immediately. She also knew she didn't want him to stop...at least not yet. If only for a moment, she yearned to feel again the sensations his stroking fingers had evoked the night before. With unconscious deliberation, she pushed caution to the farthest reaches of her mind.

"You may open every button," Kate whispered through dry lips.

There was no pause or hesitation in Trace. Swiftly, expertly, he slid the small buttons through their corresponding holes, tugging the blouse gently from beneath the waitband of her slacks to get to the last two. Then, his touch a caress, he drew the panels apart to expose her lace-covered breasts.

"Lovely." His voice a barely audible murmur,, Trace praised the perfection of her pale skin. One deft movement and the clip on the front of her bra was unfastened. Trace caught her breasts in his palms as they spilled from their lacy confines. Cupping them, lifting them, he slowly lowered his head.

"Tr-Trace?" Even as she whispered his name, Kate was arching her back in invitation.

Pausing inches from her body, Trace raised his eyes to hers. "You have beautiful breasts, Kate. Silky and exquisitely formed. Let me love them." Holding her gaze, he remained absolutely still, waiting for her response.

"Yes." A breath. A sigh. Then, as his thumbs teased the tips into readiness, a shuddering moan. "Yes, please Trace, yes!"

This time, prepared for it, the thrill that went spiraling through Kate's body at the touch of his mouth on her breasts was doubly intense and exciting. Blindly following passion's lead, she raised her hands to clasp his head, holding him to her, urging a deeper intimacy.

The flickering movement of his warm tongue sent a shaft of delight cascading along her nerves from her aroused nipples to the very tips of the fingers she pressed into his thick hair.

"Oh, Trace. Oh, Trace!" Kate was barely aware of repeating his name until his teeth gently closed around one rigid nipple. Then the throaty sound of her voice registered as she encouraged him in an impassioned plea. "Oh, Trace...yes, yes, yes!"

Without breaking the attention he was lavishing on her breasts, Trace grasped her waist and slowly slid from the settee, positioning himself on his knees on the floor between her thighs.

"You're so soft, so very soft." Trace murmured the words against her skin. "Like shimmery satin warmed before a fire."

Palms flat, fingers splayed, Trace moved his hands slowly over her rib cage, then down. When his palms brushed the waistband on her slacks he slid his hands along the material to her sides, outlining the curve of her hips before gliding inward to the front zipper.

His breath now an uneven moist cloud sensitizing her quivering flesh, Trace whispered raggedly, "May I pull the zipper, Kate?"

Why was he asking? What was he asking? Her mind spinning from the heady sensations exploding throughout her body, Kate moved her head restlessly against the back of the settee. What should she say? What should she do? Struggling against the fog of sensuality she was sinking into, she writhed agitatedly, thrusting her body artlessly into his. His reaction to the contact was instant and devastating.

"Kate!" His sharply indrawn breath was followed by a hoarse demand. "May I?" The electrifying sensation of Trace's tongue curling around one aching nipple robbed Kate of breath as well as what was left of her rationality.

"Yes! Yes! Yes!" Inside her head her words resounded like a shout; the sound that whispered through her parted lips was little more than a whimper.

As Trace continued to drive Kate senseless with his tongue, his hands were busy slipping the waistband button through its slot and releasing the zipper. With swift, economical movements he eased the material over her hips then, leaning back, off of her slender, shapely legs. Her slacks still clutched in one hand, he got to his feet. Swiftly stepping out of his jeans, he tossed both garments aside with careless abandon.

As Kate's eyes were shut tightly, she didn't see Trace divest himself of his jeans. But, in the moments he was away from her, she felt a coolness on her heated skin, and a glimmer of alarm piercing the fog of passion.

"Sweet Kate, you *are* beautiful."

The husky sound of Trace's voice closed the gap of alarm in Kate's mind. The feel of his hard thighs sliding between hers banished the growing chill. Tumbling back into the furnace of desire, Kate moaned as his hands grasped her thighs tightly to his hips, then gasped with pleasure as his fingers trailed fire from her navel to the edge of her brief panties.

Not even conscious of the fact that the soft, whimpering sounds she heard were coming from deep inside her own throat, Kate trembled as Trace slid his fingers beneath the elastic band and cried aloud when he found, then stroked, the moist heat of her femininity.

"Trace. Trace." Mindlessly murmuring his name, Kate arched her body into his touch, instinctively seeking release from the excitement and tension building to an unbearable pitch inside her.

His breathing a harsh labored rasp, Trace chanted her name like a prayer for salvation as his hands moved to grasp her sweetly rounded derriere. A visible tremor quaked through his body when Kate clasped his hips tightly with her thighs in an impassioned lover's embrace.

A wispy pink patch of nylon and a swatch of navy-blue cotton were the guardians that prevented complete unity when Trace compulsively thrust his hips into hers.

There was an instant of utter stillness as Trace held Kate's body to his with desperation. Eyes closed, he drank in the sound of her throaty murmurings while his palms absorbed the feel of her quivering flesh. Then, with a shudder, he released her and sprang to his feet.

"Oh, God!" His face a mask of strained agony, he spun around and strode unsteadily to stand before the window.

Startled, confused, and frightened by the suddenness of his violent action, Kate lay staring at him out of widening eyes, her body sprawled in a position of wild abandonment.

What had she done wrong? Had she appeared too eager for his touch? Too abandoned? Why, why had he flung himself away from her like that? Had she filled him with disgust? Unable to bear her own clamoring thoughts, she centered her attention on his hands, clenching at the sides of his tautly held body.

"Trace?" Kate whispered his name questioningly when the silence in the room stretched into long seconds. She winced in pain when his body flinched at the sound of her voice. Feeling shamed, she sat up, drawing her blouse closed protectively over her breasts.

"I...I'm sorry if I displeased you." The choking apology hurt her throat.

"You didn't displease me, Kate." Trace murmured the reassurance without turning. "The truth is, you pleased me too well." Leaning forward, he rested his forehead against the cool windowpane.

"But I don't understand!" Kate cried brokenly, drawing her legs up to clasp them with her trembling arms. "If I pleased you, why did you turn away from me like that?" Even in her agitation her gaze appreciated the sight of his masculine beauty. His deep sigh drew her gaze to the back of his well-shaped head.

"You are so unbelievably innocent!" Trace's strained laughter held the sound of splintering glass. His chest expanding with a deeply drawn breath, he turned to face her, his arousal still very much in evidence behind the flimsy covering of his briefs.

Unable to tear her gaze away from him, Kate stared, wide-eyed until, embarrassed by the realization of what she was doing, she lowered her eyes to the carpet under his feet.

"Kate, look at me," Trace commanded softly. "*Looking* at me—all of me—is nothing to be ashamed of," he chided gently when she raised her eyes hesitantly. Very deliberately he ran his gaze over her slowly. "There should be no shame in enjoying the attractions of the person you've been making love with." A tiny smile quirked the corner of his mouth. "I think you're beautiful and looking at you excites me." His quirky smile turned rueful as his gaze skimmed the length of his own body. "Obviously," he muttered.

"But then—why, Trace?" Kate blurted out in confusion.

"Honey, I've been a long time without a woman," Trace explained carefully. "A few minutes ago I was on the very edge of losing...ah...control." His lips twisted into a sardonic smile. "Had I *lost* it we'd have both been embarrassed, and my pride would have suffered for it."

Kate stared at him uncomprehendingly for a moment, then blinked as understanding dawned. What an idiot she was, she thought on a wave of fresh embarrassment. But how was she to know? Now longing to reassure him, she rushed into stuttering speech.

"Oh, Trace! I...I'm so sorry! Please forgive me. I...I didn't know!"

"Of course you didn't know," Trace inserted when she paused for breath. "I'm relieved you didn't know." He took a step toward her then stopped, a self-derisive smile curling his lips. "I wanted you very badly, Kate. I *still* want you very badly." Taking another step, he scooped his clothes from the floor. "I'm not running any more risks today." Leaning toward her he draped her slacks over her drawn-up knees. "As long as we stay here alone we're sitting on a potential powder keg." He smiled as he pulled on his jeans. "Rain or no rain, honey. I think we'll both be a lot safer if we get out of this room."

Ten minutes later, her appearance restored to at least a semblance of what it had been when she'd left her apartment that morning, Kate stood quietly beside Trace as they waited for the elevator to ascend to his floor. Not one more word had passed between them since he'd decreed that they leave his room. Now, armored by clothing and fresh makeup, Kate broke the uneasy silence.

"Trace?" she ventured tentatively.

"Hmm?" he responded mildly.

Encouraged, Kate rushed into the question that had been driving her crazy.

"You—ah—said it has been a long time since you've been with a woman." Kate paused to wet her suddenly dry lips. "Ah...well...*how* long has it been?" She stopped breathing the moment the words were out of her mouth.

Moving slowly, almost lazily, Trace turned to look at her, his eyes gleaming gemstone bright with amusement.

"A very long time, Kate." He hesitated, as if considering if he should elaborate, then he shrugged. "Since before Kathy was born, as a matter of fact."

Trace hadn't been with a woman in almost four years? The pent-up breath eased out of Kate's constricted lungs in a soundless whoosh. There were implications here that did not bear thinking about, yet Kate knew she had to obtain some answers.

"That's not very complimentary to me," Kate observed in a shaky tone. "Is it?"

"What?" All the humor fled from his eyes, leaving them as dull looking as an unpolished stone. "What are you cooking up in that inexperienced little head of yours, kid?" he demanded in an ominously soft tone.

"Well, I mean, after four years, almost *any* woman would do," Kate's throat tightened at the flash of anger that brightened his eyes, and she finished in a dry whisper, "Isn't that true?"

"No, dammit! Listen, Kate, I..."

Trace broke off as the ping announcing the arrival of the elevator car sounded. Staring ahead he followed her into the crowded elevator when the door wheezed open.

"We'll continue this conversation in the car," he muttered warningly, sliding a protective arm around her as they jostled for position.

His anger a palpable force radiating from him, Trace maintained his grip on her waist as they waited for his car to be brought to the front of the hotel. Even after they were in the car and moving, his forbidding expression warned her against breaking the silence between them.

"Now, Kate, I want you to listen very carefully to what I have to say," Trace gritted after they'd cleared the worst of the city traffic and were in more open country. "The reason I haven't been intimate with a woman all this time is not because of a lack of feminine interest; I know many willing and eager females." His lips curved cynically. "And I'm not interested in men."

"I never for one second thought you were!" Kate exclaimed in a shocked squeak.

"Thank you for that, anyway," Trace drawled, failing entirely to mask the anger still clawing at him. "I've remained celibate for one reason, and one reason only."

Suddenly swerving the car onto the shoulder bordering the highway, Trace pulled on the hand-brake then shifted on the seat to face her squarely.

"After the debacle I laughingly refer to as my marriage," he said coolly, "I made up my mind that never again would I allow myself to need or be vulnerable to any woman." Lifting an arm, he ran his fingers through his hair. "There have been times—many in number—when I've been tempted to indulge myself merely for the purpose of physical gratification." A derisive smile played over his lips. "In other words, Kate, there have been times when I ached like hell."

"Oh, Trace…"

"I'm not finished," he cut her off harshly. "Until yesterday, I've managed to work myself through those…shall I say, hard times?" He met her quick flush with a shake of his head. "By late yesterday I knew I would not be celibate too much longer," he said bluntly.

"Because of me?" Kate asked hopefully.

"Yes, Kate, because of you." Reaching out to her he stroked her cheek with his fingers, smiling when his touch drew a shiver of response from her. "I could have had a woman, a *body*, any time, Kate," he admitted without a hint of male vanity. "I chose not to. Last night, and again a short time ago, I didn't want a woman, a body, I wanted *you*, Kate, *your* body." With a final, lingering caress, Trace let his hand drop to the car seat. "I still feel the same, Kate. I will never allow myself to need you. But I do want you, as you had ample proof of earlier."

Moving so quickly Kate didn't even realize what he was doing, he leaned to her and touched his lips to hers; their mouths fused hungrily. Before the kiss could deepen, Trace pulled away from her.

"You're trembling with urgency for me, Kate," Trace murmured. "And I'm trembling, too. Eventually, we're going to be trembling in a bed, as close together as any two people ever get. I'm warning you now, in case you want to run for the hills, don't build any expectations around me, honey. I can't fulfill them."

Six

Trace was gone. Glancing away from the computer screen, Kate's gaze came to rest on the tiny watch circling her slim wrist. The digits pulsed out nine-seventeen. Trace and Kathy had reservations on a flight scheduled to depart from Philadelphia International at 9:05 A.M.

Detached from the usual workday activity and chatter around her in the large office, Kate sighed while fighting back a yawn. Feeling the effects of a sleepless night, her shoulders drooped tiredly. Dragging her gaze back to the computer she stared sightlessly at the information presented on the green screen. In her mind's eye she was reviewing the events of the preceding day. With her inner ear she heard the hard finality in Trace's voice.

"I'm warning you now, in case you want to run for the hills, don't build any expectations around me, honey. I can't fulfill them."

You know the thrill of
escaping to a world of
PASSION...SENSUALITY
...DESIRE...SEDUCTION...
and LOVE FULFILLED...

Escape again...with 4 FREE novels and

**get more great Silhouette Desire novels
—for a 15-day FREE examination—
delivered to your door every month!**

*S*ilhouette Desire offers you real-life drama and romance of successful women in charge of their lives and their careers, women who face the challenges of today's world to make their dreams come true. They are not for everyone, they're for women who want a sensual, provocative reading experience.

These are modern love stories that begin where other romances leave off. They take you *beyond* the others and into a world of love fulfilled and passions realized. You'll share precious, private moments and secret dreams...experience every whispered word of love, every ardent touch, every passionate heartbeat. And now you can enter the unforgettable world of Silhouette Desire romances each and every month.

FREE BOOKS

You can start today by taking advantage of this special offer— 4 new Silhouette Desire romances (a $9.00 Value) *absolutely FREE,* along with a Mystery Gift. Just fill out and mail the attached postage-paid order card.

AT-HOME PREVIEWS, FREE DELIVERY

After you receive your 4 free books and Mystery Gift every month you'll have the chance to preview more Silhouette Desire romances—*as soon as they are published*. When you decide to keep them you'll pay just $11.70 (a $13.50 Value), *with no additional charges of any kind and no risk!* You can cancel your subscription at any time just by dropping us a note. In any case, the first 4 books and Mystery Gift are yours to keep.

EXTRA BONUS

When you take advantage of this offer, we'll also send you the Silhouette Books Newsletter free with every shipment. Every informative issue features news on upcoming titles, interviews with your favorite authors, and even their favorite recipes.

Get a Free
Mystery Gift, too!

**EVERY BOOK YOU RECEIVE WILL BE
A BRAND-NEW FULL-LENGTH NOVEL!**

CLIP AND MAIL THIS POSTPAID CARD TODAY!

NO POSTAGE
NECESSARY
IF MAILED
IN THE
UNITED STATES

BUSINESS REPLY CARD
FIRST CLASS   PERMIT NO. 194   CLIFTON, N.J.

Postage will be paid by addressee

**Silhouette Books
120 Brighton Road
P.O. Box 5084
Clifton, NJ 07015-9956**

Escape with
4 Silhouette Desire novels
(a $9.00 Value) and get
a Mystery Gift, too!

Silhouette Desire®

Silhouette Books, 120 Brighton Rd., P.O. Box 5084, Clifton, NJ 07015-9956

Yes, please send me FREE and without obliga- tion, 4 new Silhouette Desire novels along with my Mystery Gift. Unless you hear from me after I receive my 4 FREE books, please send me 6 new Silhouette Desire novels for a free 15-day examination each month as soon as they are published. I understand that you will bill me a total of just $11.70 (a $13.50 Value), with no additional charges of any kind. There is no minimum number of books that I must buy, and I can cancel at any time. The first 4 books and Mystery Gift are mine to keep, even if I never take a single additional book.

NAME _____
(please print)

ADDRESS _____

CITY _____ STATE _____ ZIP _____

Had she begun building expectations around him, Kate wondered, automatically touching keys requesting additional information from the computer. In a secret place in her mind, had she begun weaving dreams around Trace Sinclair?

Frowning, Kate stared incomprehensibly as the data lines changed on the screen.

"Kate?"

For one thrilling instant, Kate imagined the male voice belonged to Trace. Had he somehow missed his plane, she thought fleetingly. Had he deliberately missed his plane? Hope rose like a phoenix only to die again as she swiveled around on her chair.

"Are you feeling all right, Kate?" Mr. Denunzio, the office manager, asked, a concerned frown wrinkling his forehead. "You're pale and you have dark circles under your eyes."

"I...I'm fine." Kate strove to mask the disappointment in her tone; Mr. Denunzio had always treated her with kindness and consideration. "I didn't sleep too well last night," she added truthfully.

"Too much holiday weekend?" he teased.

"I suppose so." Kate managed a weak smile thinking, too much Sinclair weekend!

"Well, don't overdo it today, and try to get a good night's sleep tonight," he advised gently. "We don't want you coming down with that flu that's been making the rounds."

"I'll take care, sir, and thank you."

With a final word of encouragement the office manager strolled off in the direction of his own office.

Though Kate ruthlessly applied herself to the business of rating insurance policies, memory flashed at odd, unsuspected moments during the day, bringing to mind brief, flickering scenes of the hours she'd spent with Trace.

The strongest of these scenes was the one that followed Trace's warning to her.

Attempting to assimilate not only what he'd said, but also what he'd left unsaid, Kate had stared at him mutely for some time; his impatience made it clear it was too long.

"Do you understand, Kate?" he'd demanded.

"Yes." Kate nodded her head once.

"Do you have any questions?"

"One," she murmured. Actually, Kate's mind seethed with questions but, since she was positive he'd prefer not to hear them, she kept them to herself.

"Well?" Trace prompted when she again fell silent.

"Will you drive me to the mall where we met yesterday?" she finally blurted.

Kate's request appeared to stun Trace. Regarding her from eyes opaque with confusion, he asked wonderingly, "You want to go shopping? Today? Sunday? In the rain?"

Kate might have laughed at his blank expression...if her eyes hadn't started to sting with the threat of tears.

"No, I don't want to shop, Trace," she assured him in a suspiciously husky tone. "I've got to get my car. It's been parked there since before noon yesterday."

Trace's brow drew together with further bewilderment. "Your car was parked there when you left the mall with Kath and me?" he exclaimed.

"Yes."

"Coffee break, Kate."

The call from the young woman who sat at the desk next to hers snapped Kate out of introspection. Frowning, she gazed up at the smiling woman.

"Boy, you're really into it today," Lisa grinned. "I haven't heard a word from you all morning."

"I'm working at staying awake." Kate's return smile lacked sparkle. "Holiday weekends tend to leave one a little groggy—don't they?" Slipping off her chair she followed the other girl to the lunch room.

"I guess that depends on how you spend the holiday weekend," Lisa laughed as she carried her coffee to an empty table. "Other than eating too much on Thanksgiving, I had a boring weekend." She eyed Kate as she seated herself across from her. "What did you do that was so very tiring?"

In a bid for time to form an answer, Kate took a deep swallow of her steaming coffee, scalding her tongue in the process. "I was Christmas shopping," she blurted with a sharply indrawn breath. "And you know how much I enjoy that!"

"Yes, I know." Lisa nodded once, then shook her head despairingly. "There are times, Kate, when I think you're an unnatural woman."

Not at all offended, Kate merely smiled and arched one questioning eyebrow.

"Well, I mean, you just aren't like other girls I know," Lisa insisted.

"Really?" Kate laughed softly. "In what way am I different?"

Lisa frowned. "You won't get angry? I mean, I don't want to hurt your feelings or anything." Her small white teeth gnawed on her lower lip. "I like you, Kate. I don't know anyone in the office that doesn't like you."

"But?" Kate prompted, curious to learn how the others felt about her.

"Well, you know," Lisa lifted her narrow shoulders in a helpless shrug. "Even though you're always dressed fashionably, you really don't seem to care about clothes like most women.''

Kate's shoulders reflected Lisa's shrug. ''That's right, I don't. Go on.''

''Well, then, there's this job,'' Lisa indicated their surroundings with a limp wave. ''To the rest of us it's just that—a job. But you seem to really love it!''

''I do,'' Kate admitted, thinking that she'd probably scream if Lisa said ''well'' one more time.

''And you don't bother with men,'' Lisa stated flatly. When Kate blinked in surprise, she added hastily. ''I mean like the rest of the single girls. I know, I know, you date occasionally, but you certainly don't seem all that interested in going out, and you never party like the girls I know.''

Kate wasn't quite sure whether to feel flattered or insulted. Every one of Lisa's assertions held validity. Other than the desire to appear presentable, clothes didn't concern Kate. She *did* enjoy her work, which was not only interesting, but financially rewarding as well. And she had never felt desperate if she found herself without a date on the weekend. As to Lisa's final point, Kate knew exactly what she meant by the term ''party.'' And, of course, it was quite true. Kate never drank more than a glass or two of wine; she did not ''do'' drugs; and she definitely didn't indulge in sexual games!

At least, she hadn't before Trace Sinclair had barged into her life! Kate writhed inwardly at the thought.

Suddenly uncomfortable, she pushed her chair back and stood up. ''Break time's over,'' she said with forced brightness.

''Now I've hurt your feelings!'' Lisa wailed.

As the conjecture about Trace had blanked all thought, Kate wasn't even sure what Lisa was talking about.

Frowning, she paused to gaze at the girl. "Hurt my feelings?" She smiled as Lisa's character analysis came rushing back. "No, you haven't. Everything you've said is true." Her smile softened with genuine amusement. "I guess I must be a female freak."

"Well, I never said that!" Lisa protested as they walked back to their desks.

Kate laughed aloud, drawing looks of surprise from several of the young women in the room.

"I know." Sliding onto her desk chair, Kate grinned. "I was only teasing."

Was she something of a female freak? The question nagged at Kate's mind intermittently throughout the remainder of the morning. At intervals, she thought about Trace and the evening they'd spent together.

Trace had driven her to where her car was parked on the large mall lot, then had followed her to her apartment building. As the rain was still coming down pretty hard, Kate had very carefully, very casually asked him if he'd like to spend the rest of the afternoon in her apartment.

"Are you crazy?" A rueful grin robbed the query of any insult. "One close call a day is about all I can handle, thank you."

Feeling somehow both inadequate and responsible, Kate gazed bleakly at the hands she was twisting in her lap. His covering hand stilled her agitated action.

"Honey, it *was* a close call," he murmured. "And all my fault." Releasing her hands, he lifted his index finger to her chin, raising her head. "Look at me, Kate," he demanded softly. When she opened her eyes, Kate's breath caught at the tenderness shining out of his eyes.

"I wanted you very badly." Trace expelled his breath with a weary sounding sigh. "Too badly. By continuing, by rushing you, I could have hurt you." The tip of his finger outlined her trembling lips. As if that visible tremor gave him pain, he groaned, "Honey, the last thing in the world I want to do is hurt you!" Dropping his hand, he sat back. "Do you understand?"

Kate nodded. She might be inexperienced, but she wasn't *that* innocent! From the things she'd read and the confidences she'd unwillingly listened to from friends, Kate was well aware that a woman's initiation to sex could be painful if not handled delicately.

Kate knew she should be feeling grateful to Trace at that moment; instead, all she felt was rejection and frustration. As if Trace could read her thoughts, he shook his head at her, smiling sadly.

"You'll be relieved when you've had time to think about it," he assured her softly. "For now, I think a change of plans is called for." Turning back to the steering wheel, he twisted the key in the ignition. "How do you feel about afternoon movies?"

"Ambivalent." Kate grimaced. "You can't hear the sound track for the kids."

"We can circumvent that." Trace slanted a teasing glance at her as he drove away from the curb. "We'll go to a film that doesn't attract a lot of kids."

Kate had loved every minute of it. Not that the movie Trace chose was great, it wasn't. In fact, it was a poorly made film. But the theater was nearly empty and they had one whole section to themselves, and Trace not only held her hand the entire time, he drew it to his lips repeatedly to press tiny, moist kisses on her palm and fingers. His kisses made it worth the price of admission.

During lunch Kate blocked the images of Trace from her mind by scrupulously attending to the conversation of the four young women she shared a table with. Since most of the talk was concerned with how the others had spent the weekend, Kate added very little to it.

By the time she went back to her desk Kate's mind boggled with the amorous exploits revealed by her co-workers. Maybe she really was something of a female freak, she reflected, amused at her shocked reaction to their frank discussion of their bedroom adventures.

Mulling over the lunchtime roundup of the weekend sexual indulgences of her table companions, Kate decided that, at almost twenty-four, she was pretty dumb. And considering the manner in which he'd left her, Trace Sinclair probably thought the same.

After leaving the theater they had gone directly to a nearby restaurant for an early dinner. For all her earlier disclaimers to the contrary, Kate was surprised to discover that she was hungry again. Strangely, considering the breakfast he'd so effortlessly consumed, Trace displayed little appetite, merely playing with the food on his plate before shoving it aside.

He drove her directly home from the restaurant, again declining her invitation to come in.

"I think not, honey." Trace smiled wryly. "Let's not tempt fate...or the devil in me." His gaze clung to her face as if to burn her likeness into his memory. "I've arranged to pick Kath up early. Our plane is schedlued to depart at 9:05."

"Give Kathy my love," Kate murmured, fighting a raspy thickness in her throat, "and tell her to write to me."

"May I write to you, too?" Trace asked, leaning across the seat to her.

Kate's heart seemed to leap at the request. Was he serious? She hoped so. "If you like," she replied wistfully.

"I do like." Moving slowly, Trace brushed his mouth over hers. "And I will." For a millisecond his mouth clung to hers. "You'd better go in now, honey," A derisive smile cut across his face as he moved away from her. "While your innocence is still intact."

Sighing, Kate glanced at her watch, groaning at the realization that only an hour and a half had passed since lunch time.

You came close to making a fool of yourself this time, Sinclair! Trace moved uncomfortably in the confines of the seat and stabbed impotently at the egg mixture in the oval plastic container. This morning his appetite was nonexistent.

Trace's normally smooth movements became awkward because of the tension that was humming through his body. His hand shook as he lifted his cup and drained the surprisingly good coffee. The instant he replaced the cup on the small tray a flight attendant materialized in the narrow aisle, glass coffeepot in hand.

"More coffee, sir?" The handsome young man smiled, his even teeth a startling white.

"Yes, thank you." A tremor ran through the long body of the plane, and Trace watched in admiration as the young man, body erect, poured the steaming liquid in a steady stream. "That's very good," Trace complimented as the attendant set the cup back on the tray.

"It goes with the job, sir." White teeth flashed again as the man moved away.

A wry smile curving his lips, Trace settled back in his seat. He could appreciate the flight attendant's insouciance. There had been times when Trace had performed not only adequately, but some claimed brilliantly, in the operating room under adverse conditions. Though he'd never put it into words, Trace's attitude mirrored the attendant's—it goes with the job.

More than one of his contemporaries had voiced the opinion that Trace was "cool under fire." A sour taste rose to sting his throat. Dr. Trace Sinclair, he thought mockingly, the cool, calm, collected whiz in the operating room, and a trembling basket case when confronted by the pale skin of a twenty-three-year-old virgin!

Shaken by the truth behind his thoughts, Trace grasped the small cup, gulping the hot brew in deep swallows. Instead of drowning the sour taste, the coffee burned his tongue and throat.

"Dammit!"

Though Trace had muttered the curse under his breath it reached the child sitting in the seat next to him.

"Don't you like your eggs, daddy?" Kathy asked, more like a concerned parent than an inquisitive child.

His set features softening, Trace turned to gaze lovingly at his frowning daughter.

"The eggs are very good, sweetheart," he replied. "I'm just not very hungry this morning." A smile easing his tight lip line, Trace indicated Kathy's breakfast with a nod of his head. "Apparently the pancakes were excellent."

Grinning impishly, Kathy glanced down at her food container, empty except for a few traces of dark maple syrup. "Yeah, they were. So were the sausages, and the cookies, and the juice." Her bright eyes sparkling with contentment, Kathy gazed up at him trustingly.

Trace didn't have the heart to chastize her about the use of the slang "yeah." Chuckling softly, he used his own napkin to wipe a dab of syrup off her chin.

"Would you like more juice?"

"Oh, no!" Kathy shook her head. "If I drink any more, I might need to go to the bathroom." Her pink lips twisted into a grimace. "And I *hate* when I have to go to the bathroom on an airplane!" She grinned when his chuckle gave way to a soft burst of laughter. "I think I'll take a nap," she said seriously. "If I sleep the time will go faster."

"Good thinking," Trace nodded solemnly. "Maybe I'll do the same."

After the breakfast trays had been cleared away Trace, following Kathy's example, released the seat to a reclining position and closed his eyes.

Though his eyes ached with a gritty sensation, Trace held out little hope of losing himself in sleep. He hadn't slept at all the night before, so why should this morning prove any different? It didn't. With conscious effort, Trace was mildly successful at relaxing the taut muscles in his body. But while his body rested, his mind raced.

What *had* happened to him?

The question had nagged at him throughout the seemingly endless night with boring regularity. Trace was almost accustomed to the question and the fact that he could find no answer to it.

Not in all the years since he'd imposed his own rule of absolute abstinence had he been so sorely tested. The realization that he'd been within a hairsbreadth of failing that test shook him to the core.

Trace was no fool. He knew, had always known, that the day would arrive when he'd consciously decide to lift the ban on physical gratification. He was a strong man, mentally as well as physically—but he *was* a man. How long could a healthy man, with an equally healthy sexual appetite, suppress the natural demands of his body?

Being a physician, Trace was aware of the effect of physical exhaustion on the libido. In consequence, he had maintained a work schedule that kept his body in a constant state of near exhaustion. His maneuver had produced two positive results. It had enhanced his reputation as a surgeon and had smothered all but the faintest twinges of sexual desire.

Those faint twinges had occurred on the rare occasions when Trace found himself in relative privacy with a woman.

Shifting his long legs to a more comfortable position in the small space between his seat and the one facing him, Trace examined the proximity as an excuse for his loss of control the afternoon before. The time required to examine the theory came to all of thirty seconds. The theory couldn't hold air, let alone be an excuse, and Trace knew it.

So, Trace charged himself scathingly, what the hell had happened to him with Kate?

Trace didn't like the answer that swirled around the edge of his consciousness. And not liking the answer, he mentally dodged it, refusing to give it substance throughout the majority of the flight west. The jet was making an approach to the landing strip when the answer formed into words that seared Trace's mind like a branding iron.

Kate Warren had happened to him.

Kate had the flu. Confined to her bed and hating every minute of it, Kate changed position for the umteenth time since waking that morning. It was Monday, the third day of her confinement, and exactly two weeks since Trace had returned to his home in San Antonio.

Trace.

Sighing softly, Kate wriggled in an effort to ease the discomfort of her aching body.

What, she wondered moodily, was Trace doing at this minute? Was he in consultation with a patient in his office? Or, perhaps, proving his expertise in the sterile environs of the operating room?

Feeling out of sorts, slightly neglected and just a little sorry for herself, Kate made no attempt to stem the tears that slid over the edge of her eyelids to roll hotly down her face.

Trace had said he would write to her; he hadn't. Had he given as much as a passing thought to her in the past two weeks? Probably not, Kate decided, sniffing loudly.

Irrationally, the thought occurred that her illness was all Mr. Denunzio's fault, simply because he'd made a point of cautioning her to take care of herself. In her more serene moments, Kate admitted to having been careless with her health while running around in the freezing rain the previous Saturday. The really galling thing was, she'd been doing, of all things, her Christmas shopping.

Christmas.

The mere thought of the swiftly approaching holiday brought a groan to Kate's lips, a frown line to her brow and, most annoyingly, a fresh surge of stinging moisture to her eyes.

On the very day before Kate finally admitted she was sick, she'd acquiesced to her mother's request that she join the family for dinner that evening to discuss plans for the holiday.

Already uncomfortable with the achey, feverish symptoms of influenza, Kate sat mutely while the rest of the family chattered incessantly around the dining-room table.

"What do you mean—you won't be here for Christmas this year?" The shocked voice belonged to Kate's mother, Arlene. She was speaking to Kate's brother, Scott.

"Now, mother," Scott's tone was soothing, but firm. "We'll be here Christmas Eve, and that's really when all the holiday action happens around here."

All the holiday action. Kate sighed wearily. Some action.

"But I still don't understand why—"

"What's to understand?" Gina Warren interrupted her mother-in-law coolly; Gina had never allowed Arlene to intimidate her. "Scott and I decided to give the kids a trip to Disney World for Christmas. We're going on an arranged tour. It leaves early on Christmas morning. It's as simple as that." Her eyes gleaming with challange, Gina sat back, fully prepared to outstare Arlene.

Arlene was fully prepared to attack in another direction—sibling loyalty.

"But, Scott!" Arlene's tone was a delicate mixture of sadness and reproach. "You'll miss your sister's birthday!"

Oh, brother! Too tired to feel more than slightly amazed, Kate turned to stare at her mother out of dull, disbelieving eyes. Since when had anybody worried about *her* birthday? Other than as an addendum to the holiday?

Scott's thoughts were obviously running along the same vein. "Mother, honestly," he expelled his breath in a sharp sigh of impatience. "We've always incorporated Kate's birthday celebration with the usual Christmas Eve festivities. Why should this year be any different?" Scott frowned. "I really don't understand what all the fuss is about. Christmas Day has never been much more than a time to recuperate from the Christmas Eve hangover.''

"Do you object, Kate?" The ostensible head of the house, Paul Warren, inserted his question in a tone that clearly said it didn't matter one way or the other what she thought.

Object? Kate tried to corral her feverish thoughts. What was the question, she wondered. Was there a question? Her sister-in-law saved Kate the effort of forming a suitable denial.

"It makes no difference whether Kate objects or not, Paul." Gina had adamantly refused to address her in-laws as mother and dad from the very beginning. Gina had also never made a pretense of putting Kate's feelings ahead of her own either. Kate admired Gina for her honesty if nothing else. "The arrangements are made. The trip is paid for." Gina lifted her head defiantly, "We leave Christmas morning."

Although Kate heard every word spoken, she was not paying much attention to the adults at the table. Her bleary gaze was busy studying the expectant expressions on the faces of her six-year-old nephew and five-year-old neice. Very little perception was needed to realize the children could almost taste Disney World.

"Oh, I think it's a wonderful plan." Kate's smile was normal, even if the reedy sound of her voice was not. "I'll bet Disney World at Christmastime will be a lot of fun."

Kate's soft observation and the children's enthusiastic response had ended the debate.

Now, feeling alternately hot and cold as the fever waxed and waned, Kate groaned aloud as the final exchange between her mother and Gina came back to haunt her. The confrontation occurred as they were all milling around at the front door—Scott and his family intent on making their way to their home in Media, Kate desperate to reach her own apartment and her bed.

"How many—ah—*close* friends will be in attendance at your Christmas Eve open house *this* year, Arlene?" Gina's tone just barely escaped being labelled a sneer.

Arlene's eyes narrowed, "I'm expecting between twenty and thirty," she informed her daughter-in-law icily.

"Oh, lovely." On that note, Gina swept out of the house, her family in tow behind her.

Lovely. Kate's thought echoed the contempt Gina had vocalized. Between twenty and thirty people, frenetic in their deisire to appear imbued with the spirit of the season, laughing too loudly, eating to excess, drinking too much.

Kate shuddered beneath the weight of her covers. What was the spirit of the holiday, anyway? Wasn't it supposed to be loving, giving and peaceful, she mused feverishly.

At that moment, weak in mind and body, Kate was inclined to agree with Trace's attitude as related by Kathy. She needed Christmas like she needed this case of the flu!

Seven

———

By Wednesday the worst of the viral infection had run its normal course through Kate's system. Though she felt weak, the fever and achiness were gone.

By early afternoon, bored to distraction, Kate pushed back the bedcovers determinedly; she'd had more than enough of staring at the ceiling. Kate was also tired of her own melancholy.

Slipping her rag-tail robe over the flannel nightgown her mother had insisted she wear, Kate slid her feet into mules and scuffed her way into the kitchen, pointedly avoiding the mirror above her dresser. She *knew* she looked like death warmed over. She didn't need confirmation.

The short trip from the bedroom to the kitchen was surprisingly tiring. The simple chore of retrieving the plastic container of beef stew her mother had brought for her the afternoon before drained Kate of her meager store of stamina. After a couple of minutes, perspiration started to dampen her forehead, neck and shoulders. Beginning to tremble, Kate gripped the refrigerator door until the bout of weakness passed.

By the time Kate transferred the stew from the container to the stove and had put the teakettle on to boil, she wasn't sure if she had the strength to eat the meal and drink the tea.

Over an hour was required to complete a process that normally would have taken less than thirty minutes. Finally, after she felt fortified by the thick stew and sweet tea, Kate cradled a fresh cup of steaming tea in her hands and made her way slowly into the living room. She understood why the doctor had adamantly insisted she not return to work until after Christmas. Merely thinking about sitting at her desk sent a quiver through her.

The phone rang as Kate sank onto the sofa in weary gratitude. Carefully placing the teacup on the coffee table next to the phone, she lifted the receiver, biting her lip in consternation at how heavy the object seemed.

"Hello?"

"You sound terrible," her mother declared in a crisp tone. "Are you feeling worse?"

"No, mother," Kate sighed. "Actually, I'm feeling much better. I just got myself something to eat and it tired me out." Even Kate could hear the amazement in her tone. "The beef stew was very good, mother." Studying her trembling fingers with a frown, Kate brought the cup to her lips to sip the hot tea.

"Well, of course it tired you!" Arlene exclaimed in exasperation. "Kate, fighting the influenza infection has depleted your body. You must not overdo or you'll have a relapse."

"Yes, mother." Kate smiled wryly; there was more pedantry in her mother's tone than parental concern. "I promise I won't overdo and have a relapse."

"I should hope not," Arlene snapped. "It would ruin your holiday."

What? Kate shook her head. The holiday! Oh, brother! Aloud she murmured, "I'll be back in fighting shape for the holiday, mother."

"Not if you don't take care of yourself," Arlene retorted.

"I'm going to rest now, mother," Kate said, distractedly glancing at her hand, which was beginning to tremble from the weight of the receiver. "I promise that except for an emergency, like a fire, I won't move from the sofa." Kate silently congratulated herself on the return of her sense of humor; maybe she would live, after all!

Arlene was not amused. "Your sense of humor escapes me! There isn't one thing funny about the possibility of a fire." Her sigh conveyed years of impatience. Her pause invited apology; Kate declined. When Arlene spoke again her voice was sharp with annoyance. "I'll stop by again after work."

"That won't be necessary, mother. I'll be able to manage by myself now." Kate closed her lids over a sudden sting in her eyes. Though she appreciated her mother's evening visits since Sunday, she faced the fact that they had been made out of a sense of duty, not real affection. "This *is* your bridge night, isn't it?" Kate asked tiredly.

"Yes. We're having a little wine and cheese afterward and exchanging small gifts," Arlene sighed. "But, I really feel I should stop by your place and get you a meal."

The "I feel I should" hurt Kate more than if her mother had bluntly told her she didn't want to come. Two warm, salty tears rolled down Kate's cheeks quickly followed by a gathering trickle.

"I had a meal." Kate managed a steady tone. "You and dad go and have a good time. I'll be fine."

"Well, if you insist." Relief was evident in Arlene's tone; the decision had been taken from her. "Now you rest, Kate. I'll call you tomorrow and, oh, yes, I brought in your mail yesterday. It's on the corner of the coffee table."

After replacing the receiver, which now felt like it must weigh at least fifty pounds, Kate closed her eyes and sipped at the rapidly cooling tea. Concentrating on collecting her rattled emotions, she momentarily forgot about the mail.

Why, she chided herself, did she let her parents' disinterest—or forced interest—upset her anymore? Hadn't she faced the reality of their life-style and total self-interest long ago? Kate sighed raggedly. If she ever, ever had a family of her own, she vowed, she'd smother them in love and caring! There would never be any doubt about how *she* felt!

Setting the remains of the tea aside, Kate stretched out on the sofa. The instant her weary body was prone a haunting vision of the last time she'd reclined in exactly the same spot rose to torment her mind. On that previous occasion she had not been alone—not in the apartment, not on the sofa. An excitingly hard male body had warmed her outside; an enticing male mouth had scorched her inside.

Throughout the length of her bout with the flu, Kate had relived the hours she'd spent with Trace. In disjointed, fever-induced scenes their meager time together swirled through her memory in fragmented bits and pieces. Prisoner to the accelerated flow of mental images, Kate had cried his name aloud several times. Now, lucid, she did the same.

"Oh, Trace."

With a sigh that was more of a groan, Kate curled into the warmth of her tattered robe. Immediately, the essence that was uniquely Trace captured her imagination, and he was there with her, enveloping her with his strength.

Kate's slender body quivered as she recalled all the clamoring passion Trace had evoked in her. Weakened by her illness, she lay helpless against memory's onslaught, yearning for the low, enticing sound of his voice, the gentle caress of his hands and, yes, the fulfilling presense of his body, banishing the emptiness in hers.

Depleted in spirit as well as strength, Kate moaned with the certainty growing in her mind. Against all reason, she was very much afraid that she was falling in love with Trace Sinclair. Biting her lip, she prevented the moan from becoming a sob.

How had it happened so quickly, Kate agonized, locking her arms around herself. She hardly knew the man, and yet it was as if she'd known him forever.

Infatuation! Yes, that's what it was; that's what it had to be, Kate argued inwardly. It simply was not possible to fall in love with a man she'd known for such a short period of time.

Infatuation was harmless, especially when the man was almost half a continent away. Heaving a sigh of relief, Kate sat up and reached for the mail that had accumulated since Monday.

There were several business-size envelopes which Kate shoved aside. There were the usual pieces of junk mail which Kate ignored. There was also a stack of greeting-card-sized envelopes. Placing the stack on her lap, Kate settled back into the corner of the sofa to open her cards in comfort.

There were several "get well" cards from the girls she worked with, including a rather humorous one from Lisa, the girl who sat at the desk next to Kate's. There was also a large card, signed by every one of the women that worked in Kate's office. There were three Christmas cards—one from a friend Kate had known since grade school, one from her brother and sister-in-law and one that bore a return address that made Kate's heart skip a beat.

Kate had sent a Christmas card containing a brief note to the same address the week before. Trace had given her the address; it was for his home outside San Antonio. Both the return address in the left-hand corner and her own in the center of the envelope had been typed.

With shaking fingers Kate tore open the envelope and withdrew the expensive greeting card. Her eyes swiftly skimmed the words that wished her seasons' greetings from the Alamo, and the illuminated scene of the famous shrine. Flipping the card open, Kate ran her gaze over the typed message inside.

I miss you, Kate. I wish you could be here for Christmas, but daddy said you have a family and plans of your own. But I pray every night that I get what I asked Santa Claus for for Christmas.
    Love and kisses,

                                            Kathy

A soft smile curved Kate's lips and tears welled in her eyes as she stared at the painstakingly printed name beneath the one someone had typed for the child. Had Trace typed the message for Kathy, Kate wondered bleakly. Did he know that his daughter had sent return greetings to the young woman who'd cared for the child while she was lost?

The very real possibility that Trace Sinclair hadn't given as much as a single thought to her since his return to San Antonio caused a twist of near anguish in Kate's chest and mind. Cradling the card to her heart, Kate closed her eyes and let the tears of longing and loneliness slide unheeded down her face.

The jarring sound of the doorbell shattered the cocoon of misery Kate was sinking into. Kathy's card clutched in her hand, Kate rose shakily and walked unsteadily to the door.

A middle-aged man stood in the hallway, a large, tissue-wrapped flower arrangement in one hand, the index finger of his other hand poised to push the bell button again.

"Miss Warren?" he inquired politely.

"Yes."

"These are for you, miss." The man placed the arrangement in Kate's hands then, as if he was in a hurry to get on with his deliveries, he turned away.

"Wait!" Kate called, if weakly. "I'll get a tip for you."

"Not necessary, miss," the man said kindly, already striding down the hall. "Enjoy."

Maybe the flowers were from Trace!

The idea struck, hopefully if irrationally, as Kate closed the door. As she crossed the room, she realized that Trace would have no way of knowing that she'd been ill. Still, the flowers *could* be a combined thank you and Christmas gift.

And there really *could* be a Santa Claus, Kate thought dejectedly moments later, biting her lip as she stared at the tiny florists' card, signed simply: Speedy recovery from the benefit fund of Coast To Coast Insurance Co.

Of course, Kate knew about the office kitty. It had been set up for this type of occasion—sending "get well" flowers to a sick coworker. Kate contributed to the fund on a regular basis. And it wasn't as if she didn't appreciate the cheery, seasonal bouquet.

Silently chiding herself for her deep sense of disappointment, Kate discarded the tissue and made room on the low coffee table for the floral arrangement. After positioning the flowers, Kate scooped up the business-size envelopes she'd brushed aside to make room for the bouquet.

Bills. There were four of the long envelopes and, sighing, Kate proceeded to tear open the first one. She was withdrawing the enclosed sheet of paper when her gaze skimmed, then became riveted on, the return address on the next long envelope.

Casting the envelope she was holding aside, she lifted the next one with trembling fingers. The return address had been imprinted and looked very professional. It declared that the contents of the envelope came from Trace M. Sinclair, M.D. and gave what Kate had to assume was the address of his medical office.

If it's a check in payment for looking after Kathy, I'll rip it in half and send it back, Kate thought forlornly, almost afraid to open it. As her hands absently smoothed the envelope's heavy, quality paper, she mused on Trace's middle initial. What did the M stand for? Michael? Mitchell? Martin, perhaps?

Deciding the M stood for Michael simply because she preferred it, Kate turned the envelope over and carefully slid her fingernail under the flap. Managing to unseal the flap without a single tear, she slowly withdrew a small square of paper, folded in half. By its size, the single sheet of paper was obviously not a check. A long, shuddering sigh whooshed through Kate's lips as she slipped her thumb between the fold and flipped the paper open.

Her eyes widening in surprise, Kate noted that the sheet of paper had been torn from a regulation prescription pad; the letterhead at the top was identical to the one on the envelope. A choking gasp tightened her throat as her gaze dropped to the four words written in a bold slash across the center of the paper.

Come to Texas, Kate.

That was it. There was no salutation, no signature, just the exact same words Trace had repeated to her several times in the scant two days they were together. Just— "Come to Texas, Kate."

The paper wavered in her trembling hand, then the script blurred. Sobbing softly, Kate was positive she could hear Trace, his voice teasing, coaxing as he murmured the enticing invitation.

Lord, he was tired! Sighing, Trace leaned back into the plush padding of his high-backed desk chair. Closing his eyes he absently massaged the bunched muscles in his neck.

Long fingers digging rhythmically into the tension-tightened muscles and tendons, Trace slowly worked his hand along the curve of his neck to his right shoulder. Perhaps he should take the time to go to the health club and have a professional rubdown, he thought, wincing when the tips of his fingers dug into a particularly tender spot.

Yeah, sure...but when? Trace scoffed at his own idea.

Right now, he had fifteen minutes all to himself. Trace grimaced; fifteen minutes to rest before Maggie, his nurse-receptionist, ushered his next scheduled patient into his consulting office.

The grueling pace Trace had maintained since his return from Philadelphia over three weeks ago had been killing; at that moment he felt more dead than alive. And, as if the workload he'd taken on hadn't been enough, Trace had spent many precious hours searching the stores for gifts he *hoped* Kathy would like. Since all Kathy would say in response to his repeated requests to know what she wanted for Christmas was, "Santa Claus knows what I want," at best his selections had been hit or miss.

"This whole holiday craziness is a pain in the—"

"I just received notice that your next appointment, Mr. Craig, will be delayed, doctor." Maggie's no-nonsense voice cut across Trace's muttered imprecation against the holiday via the office intercom.

"How long delayed?" Trace shot back irritably.

"His wife said ten minutes, fifteen at the outside," Maggie informed tonelessly.

"Is the patient due to follow Mr. Craig here yet?"

"No, sir."

Trace heaved an impatient sigh. "Okay, we wait." Smoothing the ruffles of annoyance from his tone, he added, "Would you bring me a cup of coffee, Maggie?"

"Certainly."

The intercom went silent. Less than three minutes later Maggie entered the room quietly on rubber-soled shoes, a coffee mug in one hand and a small plate in the other.

"I thought you might like a piece of baklava," she murmured, sliding the plate onto the desk in front of Trace. "It's fresh. I picked it up on my way to the office this morning."

A twitching smile betrayed the stern expression Trace leveled on his amply endowed, middle-aged right arm.

"Baklava?" he groaned, shifting his gaze to the honey and walnut pastry. "In the middle of the day? Are you trying to sabotage my waistline?"

Maggie's snort of ridicule bespoke long familiarity with her employer. Arching one gray-tinged eyebrow, she swept his figure with bright, intelligent eyes.

"I seriously doubt your waistline will be in any danger from this one small pastry triangle," Maggie said dryly. "In fact, as a professional, I'd hazard a guess that your waistline has decreased by some two inches within the past few weeks."

"You're a treasure, Maggie," Trace drawled. "But you do have an annoying tendency to nag."

"That being the case," Maggie retorted, moving silently to the door, "I'm going to offer some unsolicited advice. You must slow down, doctor. You're losing weight...and you're beginning to resemble a haunted shadow."

Trace gave a choking laugh around the bite of pastry he was chewing, "a haunted shadow!" Swallowing carefully, he shook his head. "Where did you come up with that?" A teasing light brightened his tired eyes. "Have you been watching some late-night ghost movies on TV?"

"I never watch TV and you know it," Maggie denied calmly. "But I do tend to watch you. I have for the entire two hundred and twenty years I've been with you."

"Is that what it's been? Doesn't seem a day over two hundred and nineteen," Trace observed mockingly

Then, his expression sobering, he assured softly, "I'm all right, Maggie."

"You're not, you know." She opened the door, then paused to glance back at him, her face set into lines of concern. "You need to be pampered a little bit by a good, willing woman." Her tone made it clear that she wasn't teasing.

"I don't *need* anything, Maggie." A chill had invaded Trace's tone. "Least of all a woman, willing or otherwise."

"Whatever you say, doctor," Maggie smiled sadly. "You have approximately twenty-five minutes. Try to relax a little." With an almost imperceptible sigh, she closed the door quietly behind her.

Trace stared at the wood surface with a wry smile on his lips. Maggie addressed him as "doctor" in that particular tone only when she was put-out with him. Shrugging, he turned back to the baklava and coffee. Twenty-five whole minutes, he marveled. Whatever will I do with all that free time?

What Trace did, while chewing pastry and sipping coffee, was remember instances he had convinced himself were better forgotten.

A willing woman. Unknowingly, Trace's mouth curved sensuously. Kate had been willing. Closing his eyes, he rolled her name around in his mind. Kate. Kate of the alluring smoke-colored eyes and hair the shiny hue of licorice extract. Kate of the clinging arms and the moist mouth, eager to learn. Kate. Kate of the soft, laughing voice and virginal innocence. Kate. Kate. Kate.

Sudden passion, hot and intense surged through Trace's body. Muffling a groan, he clasped the mug with both hands, as if hanging on for dear life.

God, he wanted to possess that woman!

He didn't *need* Kate, Trace assured himself confidently. But he sure did want her!

Settling into his chair, Trace took a deep swallow of the lightly creamed coffee. Actually, he mused, Kate has a lot going for her. She's intelligent, beautiful, has a terrific sense of humor and a sweetly exciting body. A flashing image of her body, her pale naked skin gleaming in invitation, drew a fine film of moisture to his brow.

Maybe he should have taken her when he had the opportunity. No, of course he couldn't have taken her then; he'd been too hot, too ready. But, damn, if he'd have taken her he wouldn't be sitting here now, getting the sweats from simply thinking about her! Oh, no, he'd more than likely be sitting here really hating himself...and still wanting her anyway!

The silent argument was a familiar one to Trace. He'd had it with himself a dozen times since returning from the east coast. A smile of derision quirked his lips. The last time he'd engaged in that inner debate, he'd ended by tearing a sheet off his prescription pad to use as an invitation to Kate to join him in Texas. Naturally, Kate had made no response.

You're a fool, Sinclair, Trace informed himself mockingly. Did you actually think Kate would hop on the first plane west after receiving an invitation that sounded more like a command?

She might have at least sent me a Christmas card; she sent one to Kathy.

Hearing the sound of his own thoughts echoing inside his head, Trace straightened abruptly in his chair. Will you listen to yourself, he demanded silently. You sound exactly like Kathy when she's into her best whining routine! This has got to stop, Sinclair. Kate Warren is a woman, like other women...nothing less, but nothing more either. Get to work and forget her.

Even as Trace issued the advice he was reaching for the prescription pad at the corner of his desk.

By the week before Christmas Kate had a very bad case of cabin fever. Although she had always felt comfortable in her apartment, after two weeks of being confined to the three rooms and miniscule bathroom, she was becoming very antsy.

Despite the fact that merely making the short trip to her mailbox in the lobby left her shaking with weakness, Kate decided she had to get out, if only for an hour.

As Kate dressed to go out, she attempted to convince herself this trip really *was* necessary. Her food supply had dwindled, so a trip to the supermarket was a must. And there were still a few items on her Christmas list to be purchased.

Recalling the usual family plans for the holiday brought a grimace to Kate's soft lips. One of these years, she promised herself for perhaps the thousandth time, she would take her vacation weeks in December and run away—if she could find a place where she wouldn't be saturated with the trappings of the season. Kate knew there were such places, but she also knew that the cost of running to them would be prohibitive.

Deciding to keep her priorities straight, Kate tackled the supermarket first. Three overstuffed shopping bags later, Kate stumbled into her apartment, groaning softly and perspiring profusely. Trembling with fatigue, she stashed the perishables haphazardly into the refrigerator, swallowed the vitamin tablet her doctor had recommended, then fell fully clothed on the bed, consigning the Christmas shopping to another day.

On the morning of the twenty-second of December Kate convinced herself she was ready to face the crowds of last-minute shoppers.

The day was mild and bright, the sky such an intense blue that it cheered her spirits just by looking at it. Kate could have chosen any one of several different malls to shop in. Without conscious thought she found herself parking on the lot of the mall where she'd met first Kathy, then Trace.

Deciding she must have latent masochistic tendencies, Kate headed for the tall tree in the center of the mall like a homing pigeon. Her eyes shadowed with longing, she watching as a few late stragglers, their small faces uncertain, tentatively approached by now a weary looking man garbed in red velvet and fake white fur.

In her mind's eye Kate held a sharply defined image of a small girl, her blond curls shimmering from the excitement shaking through her tiny body, her eyes sparkling with expectation, her sweet face glowing with wonder.

Kate turned from the scene abruptly when her eyes began to sting. There had been no more notes from Kathy, nothing from Trace, not even a Christmas card.

Shaking herself mentally, Kate strode purposely away from the site of her first encounter with Kathy. The incident was over, both the child and the father were out of her life. It's just as well, she reasoned, ignoring the way everything was growing blurry. She'd begun to spin dream castles while convalescing; now it was time to get back to the real world.

Discovering she felt much stronger than just the day before, Kate made a day of her shopping. She had lunch in one of the many restaurants located inside the mall, but not the one that she'd taken Kathy to.

By midafternoon Kate had drawn a check mark on every item that remained on her list; she even had most of the gifts wrapped. She was making her way to the exit when her glance was snagged by a small jewelry store display window. Reluctantly, battling the sentimental emotion that urged her forward, Kate walked to the showcase to stare at the item that had caught her eye.

Cast in a glowing matte pewter, the piece displayed was a replica of the Liberty Bell. It was approximately three inches high and four inches wide. A soft sigh of defeat whispered through Kate's lips as she studied the exquisite detail of the piece. Even as resistence tightened her slender body, she turned to walk into the shop. She was going to buy it. Even if she never gave it to him, she simply *had* to buy it for Trace.

Oddly, purchasing the bell, then waiting while the clerk gift wrapped it, drained Kate to the point of exhaustion. On trembling legs, she walked slowly to her car; with trembling arms and hands, she carefully drove home.

Unceremoniously dropping her coat, purse and other packages onto the chair just inside the door, Kate cradled the brightly packaged bell in one hand and clasped her mail in the other as she crossed the room to the sofa.

Setting the stack of mail aside for the moment, Kate set the bell on the coffee table, then sat staring at it, her bottom lip caught between her teeth.

Did she have the nerve to mail the gift to him, Kate mused. She knew full well Trace's opinion of the holidays; in many ways his opinion coincided with her own. If she did send it to him, would he frown upon opening it? Maybe even send it back to her, along with a sarcastic note? Kate's teeth sank deeper into her lip. Perhaps she'd be better off stashing it in the back of her closet—and hopefully forgetting it.

Yet, in many ways the little bell seemed to symbolize and represent aspects of Trace's character. The traits of independence, confidence, pride and strength were as ingrained in Trace as they were in the symbol of liberty. And, as the bell had been cracked with its first peel, Trace's pride and ego had figuratively been cracked by his first emotional commitment.

Smiling sadly at her own whimsy, Kate smoothed the small package with trembling fingers. Oh, yes, the bell was definitely for Trace...even if she never gave it to him.

Swallowing against a sudden thickness in her throat, Kate pulled her hand from the gift and reached for the mail. Disinterestedly shuffling through the stack her eyes froze on one long business envelope. The return address was the same as on the one she'd received the week before. Her breathing unsteady, Kate tore the envelope open and withdrew the small, folded sheet from a prescription pad. And, as on the one the previous week, the paper contained just four words.

Come to Texas, Kate.

Eight

A gentle smile on his lips, Trace quietly shut the door to Kathy's bedroom. It was the second night in a row that he'd made it home in time not only for dinner but to put Kathy to bed as well.

His smile twisting slightly, Trace strolled into his home office. Due to the excitement of the swiftly approaching holiday Kathy had proved a bouncing handful on both nights. Yet still, when questioned, all the child would say was, "Santa knows what I want."

Going directly to the beautifully carved credenza, Trace splashed whiskey into a glass then dropped in two ice cubes. While sipping appreciatively, he walked to the large desk in front of a window that overlooked Kathy's play area in the yard.

Savoring the smoky flavor of the whiskey, Trace propped his feet on the edge of the desk and let his head rest on the back of his chair. It had been a slow week because, as usual, none of his patients would consider surgery the week before Christmas except in an emergency.

For himself, Trace was in mental conflict over the amount of free time he suddenly found himself with. Trace was all too aware that he was pretty much an absentee father. So, on the one hand he was grateful for the opportunity to be with Kathy. Yet, on the other hand, he didn't relish the quiet moments after Kathy was asleep. The quiet was far too inducive to thoughts, thoughts that persisted in traveling east to a woman with vibrant black hair, and smoke-colored eyes, and lips the memory of which could drive a rational man to drink.

Self-mockery turned his eyes cynical. Gazing into the amber whiskey, Trace cautioned himself against having more than one drink; although he had no surgery scheduled the next day, there was always the possibility of an emergency arising. Just one more day, then he would be free until after Christmas; it was his associates' turn to work a holiday.

"Will there be anything else tonight, doctor?"

Dropping his feet to the floor, Trace swiveled his chair toward the doorway. His housekeeper of six years, Inez Peranza, stood in the threshold, her expression one of patient attention.

"No, thank you." A teasing smile hovered around Trace's mouth. "Is the TV movie a good one tonight?" he asked softly.

"*Si*," Inez nodded her silver-streaked head. "The film *Valdes is Coming* is being shown again."

"Really?" Trace was no longer teasing. "Maybe I'll tune it in. I liked that film."

"I know," Inez grinned, revealing teeth that were still in excellent condition, even after sixty-odd years. "Have a good evening, doctor."

"Thanks, Inez," Trace sighed. "Good night. Enjoy the movie."

Trace's eyes fell on his desk phone as the door closed with a muffled click. When he'd walked into the house late that afternoon, Inez had handed him two phone messages. One message had been from his mother, the other from his ex-mother-in-law. After greeting Kathy, Trace had come to the office. Taut with concern, he'd dialed his parents' number in Hawaii. When his mother answered, he'd bypassed the usual greeting to get to the point.

"Is dad all right?" Though his voice had an acquired note of professional calm, Trace felt fear crawl in his guts. His father, Michael T. Sinclair, had been a noted heart specialist before suffering a massive coronary two years previously. After an almost spectacular recovery, Michael decided he'd rather live than tempt fate by pursuing his career. Within six months of his decision to retire, Michael had disposed of his fashionable Houston home and had whisked his wife to Hawaii. Trace's parents had planned to fly to San Antonio to spend the holidays with their only child and grandchild. Before his mother spoke, Trace knew something had happened to interfere with their plans.

"Dad had a very slight heart attack this morning, Trace." Kathryn Sinclair said bluntly, complimenting her son's intelligence both as a man and a physician. "Doctor Cassiday assured me that Michael is in no danger," she went on firmly. "But he also stressed the inadvisability of a long trip at this time."

"Of course," Trace inserted coolly, releasing a silent sigh of relief. "Kath and I will miss you, but dad's health is more important than the holidays."

Trace had talked with his mother for a few more minutes, then had called Kathy to the phone. Well aware of the opinion both his parents had always had of Annette, Trace didn't mention his former wife's threat of a child custody battle in the near future.

The second message he'd set aside until after Kathy was in bed for the night; the last thing Trace needed was to have the child upset and, intuitively, Trace knew he wasn't going to be happy with whatever it was that Ruth wanted. He dialed her phone number.

Trace's intuition was absolutely correct. Using the same direct approach as his mother had, Ruth came to the point immediately.

"Trace, I realize it's asking a great deal," she began slowly, then rushed on, "but could we have Kathy here for Christmas Day?"

"What?" Trace half laughed, too stunned to believe he'd heard her clearly.

"Oh, Trace, please, just hear me out before you refuse," Ruth hurried on. "As you know, Annette's brother Carl has been working in Japan for his company for over four years now. His twin sons have never experienced an American Christmas."

"I know all that, Ruth," Trace said impatiently. "But, I don't see what that—"

"Carl and his family came home yesterday," Ruth interrupted breathlessly. "And, well, we'd like to have a real family Christmas for them—with all the children together." She paused, very briefly, then continued. "Trace, you've never kept your aversion to the holiday a secret."

"That doesn't mean I don't want to spend it with my daughter," Trace retorted.

"I know, I'm sorry," Ruth murmured contritely, then softly, persuasively, "Trace, I'm being very selfish but, just once, I'd like to have all my grandchildren here on Christmas."

Trace was still staring at the beige phone ten minutes after he'd disconnected. Sighing, he pushed back his chair and carried his glass to the kitchen. It was really a pity he was so fond of Ruth, he thought tiredly. If he'd have liked her less, he might have been able to refuse her request. As it was, now he'd have to pull some strings to get a flight east on Christmas Eve.

Flicking off lights as he went, Trace secured the house for the night. On his way upstairs, he stopped at the archway to the living room and reached for the light switch on the wall. His gaze rested a moment on the six-foot balsam tree framed by the picture window at the front of the house. The tree was beautifully bedecked, waiting for the brightly wrapped gifts to shelter under its branches.

Touching the switch, Trace turned for the stairs, his lips tight, his expression cynical.

"Yes, indeedy," he muttered derisively. "And a Merry Christmas to you too, Sinclair."

Kate held the jewel-toned velvet pants suit in midair and ran a critical glance over its classic lines. Had the spilled drink spoiled it, or could the dry cleaner save its life? Examining the large, stiffened spot more closely, she swore softly. She really should have followed the urge that cautioned her against wearing the suit the night before; she was in a position to know how very sloppy her parents' Christmas Eve "gatherings" could get.

Sighing resignedly, she carefully folded the suit and placed it on her bedroom chair before turning back to her closet. Removing a silky men's-style shirt from a hanger, she slipped it on and tucked it into the narrow jeans that hugged her slim hips; on Christmas Day it didn't matter what she wore to visit her parents.

While applying a light brush of peaock-blue eyeshadow that matched the color of her shirt, Kate did a mental postmortem of the Christmas Eve party.

As usual, her parents' split-level home was crowded to bursting with their "intimate" friends of the moment— half of whom Kate didn't know...or want to know for that matter.

And, per usual, the drinks, of all varieties, were flowing like a rain-swollen river. By the time Kate arrived several of the guests were already unfurling their fourth sheet to the wind.

And, as always, Kate felt like a stranger in the house she'd grown up in. And a disgusted stranger at that.

Christmas carols blared from the stereo, voices were raised as people shouted to one another from room to room, and at least a half-dozen children ran around, seemingly in circles, screaming excitedly.

All in all, Kate mused, it was the same old general mess. The absolute topper of the evening for Kate was being backed into a corner by a man easily as old as her father, then having the slob spill his drink down the length of one leg of her pantsuit.

Well, it wasn't a complete disaster, Kate concluded, grinning at herself in the mirror. Being baptized by whiskey and water had given her the perfect excuse to leave.

And now she was going back. Kate's grin faded as her lips curved down. She knew exactly what she'd be walking into. Although the house would have been tidied by now, Kate knew both her parents would be sleepy and dull, even though her father would make a show of Christmas cheeriness.

Kate shuddered. It was always the same. Noting the time was 10:22, she stuck her arm into the closet and withdrew her coat, reluctantly slipping it on as she walked out of the bedroom. She was reaching for the doorknob when the phone rang. Grateful for any delay, however brief, she crossed the room to the coffee table and lifted the receiver.

"Hello, Merry Christmas." Kate wasn't sure why she'd given the greeting. She certainly didn't feel very merry.

"Hello, Kate."

"Trace?" For an instant Kate went completely blank. Then everything accelerated. Her heart beat faster, her breathing became shallow, her mind whirled. "Where are you?" she cried.

"A few blocks away," he said quietly, "in a phone booth." Trace was silent for a moment, then he said quickly, "I don't want to interfere with any plans you may have, but do you have time for a cup of coffee with me?"

"Time? Of course I have time!" And if I didn't I'd have time anyway, Kate added silently.

"Good." Trace expelled his breath audibly. "I'll pick you up in a few minutes. Okay?"

"Yes, I'll be waiting." As she hung up, Kate's hand bumped the elegantly wrapped package that contained the pewter bell. Without giving herself time to consider, she scooped it up and slid it into her capacious shoulder bag.

Trace brought the rented Ford to a gliding stop along the curb as Kate ran down the three steps to the sidewalk. Leaning across the seat he opened the passenger door for her as she circled the front of the car.

Kate ran an encompassing glance over Trace as she slid into the car. He looked tired, thinner, and somehow disillusioned...and altogether wonderful.

"Hello," she said softly, smiling tentatively.

"Hello, yourself." The lines radiating from the corners of his eyes deepened with his return smile. "You look like every man's dream of the perfect Christmas present," Trace said solemnly.

"*You* look like you've been working too hard," Kate replied candidly, contentedly joining him when he laughed easily.

"Well, now that we've exchanged compliments," Trace drawled, "shall we see if we can find a place that's open on holidays?"

"I know of only one," Kate said thoughtfully. "The convenience store out on the highway."

Putting the car in gear, Trace drove away. "Just tell me when to turn, honey."

Less than five minutes later, Trace parked the car in front of the convenience store. "You were right," he observed dryly, indicating a large sign in the window promising that the store would be open on Christmas Day from 9:00 A.M. till 6:00 P.M. Thrusting his door open, Trace slanted a quick glance at her.

"Don't go away, honey, I'll be back in a minute with our Christmas breakfast." Slamming the door, he strode into the store.

It was after ten-thirty. Hadn't Trace eaten anything, Kate wondered. And where was Kathy, anyway? For all his talk of disliking the holiday, Kate would have bet a month's salary that Trace would play out the role of merrymaker for Kathy's sake. Suddenly worried, she waited impatiently for him to return.

When Trace came back to the car he was grasping a brown paper bag by the top while balancing the bottom of it in the palm of his other hand. As he opened the door, Kate shot her question at him.

"Where's Kathy, Trace?"

"With her grandparents," Trace said tersely, sliding carefully into the car. "It's a long story. I'll tell you about · it while we eat."

Setting the bag on the seat between them, Trace dipped his hand inside and withdrew two plastic-wrapped, iced buns. Dropping the pastries into Kate's lap, he plunged his hand inside again and retrieved two Styrofoam cups of coffee. After handing one of the cups to her, he removed both the lids. Steam rose from the cups, filling the interior of the car with the aroma of freshly brewed coffee.

"Mmm, smells delicious," Kate murmured, inhaling deeply.

"Yeah, the first of the day always does." Trace started to raise the cup to his lips then, hesitating briefly, he held it aloft. "Thank heaven for Seven-Eleven," he drawled, tentatively sipping the hot brew.

A shiver of alarm swept through Kate. There was a weariness in Trace that went far deeper than the surface signs revealed; a weariness that had more to do with the spirit than the body.

Gently blowing on her coffee, Kate studied him over the rim of her cup. Though Trace would probably rather die than show it, he was obviously hurting—at least it was obvious to Kate because suddenly, she was hurting too. Impulsively, she made an offer to help.

"What's bothering you, Trace?" she asked softly, her tone relaying her willingness to listen if he cared to unburden himself.

Trace's crooked smile acknowledged her offer. "This whole holiday razzmatazz," he replied sardonically. He was quiet a moment, observing her contemplatively, then he shrugged. "I never thought I'd feel lonely on Christmas." He smiled derisively. "Yet, lonely was exactly what I felt this morning. I...ah...appreciate the company, Kate."

A sharp pain shot through Kate's chest making it almost impossible for her to breathe. Trace hadn't shut his emotional door on her—he'd slammed it in her face. Dredging a smile from the tattered edges of her pride, Kate said flippantly. "Oh, you mean I'm a port in the holiday storm?" Glancing down, she toyed with the wrapped pastries. "Happy to oblige."

"Dammit!" Trace muttered the exclamation as he reached out to raise her chin with hard fingers. "That's not what I meant!"

"What did you mean, Trace?" Head up, Kate faced him squarely. "What exactly do you expect of me? Am I supposed to just sit quietly and keep you company?"

"Kate..." Trace began.

"Or," Kate went on relentlessly, "did you hope I'd invite you into my apartment and my bed?" Kate sniffed, but refused to allow the threatening tears release. "I must admit, that would be one way to take the edge off loneliness."

"Kate!" Trace reflexively tightened his hold on her chin. "Kate, will you stop this and listen?"

"To what?" Kate shouted. "You're not saying anything!"

"I might if you'd shut up!" he shouted back. "What's wrong with you?"

Blinking rapidly, Kate jerked away from his fingers to stare through the windshield. "I'm afraid," she breathed tightly. "I'm so afraid."

"Afraid?" Trace repeated blankly. Then, incredulously, "Kate! You don't really believe I'd ask to see you this morning to force myself on you?"

"No!" Kate shook her head sharply, "Of course not!"

Trace expelled a sigh of frustration. "Then why are you afraid?" Capturing her chin again, he turned her head. "Honey, tell me."

"You're not going to like hearing it," Kate warned, smiling at the wary look that entered his eyes. Her gaze locked to his, she said clearly, "I'm afraid I'm falling in love with you, Trace."

With an outward calm that masked the uncertainty and hope battling within her, Kate watched as Trace absorbed the shock of her statement. There was a sudden alert wariness about him that touched a chord in her, making her hurt for him even while she was hurting so very badly herself. This man had been raked over the coals of love; every tiny nuance about him warned that he would not willingly step into that fire again. The cynical smile that briefly feathered his lips confirmed Kate's conjecture.

"Do you know what love is, Kate?" Trace asked too softly. "Have you been in love before?"

"No," Kate responded simply.

"I suspected as much." Trace nodded once. "If we had the time, I'd tell you about love, kid," he muttered, squashing the empty cup and dropping it into the paper bag.

Kate's hesitation was barely noticeable. "I have all day." Without conscious thought, she handed her half full cup to him. When he frowned in question, she smiled, "You finish it. I've had my breakfast this morning."

"I wasn't questioning the coffee," Trace said impatiently. "What do you mean you have all day? You were obviously dressed to go out when I called—weren't you?"

"Yes, to my parents' house," she admitted. "But it won't cause any problems if I call and tell them I'm not coming." At the questioning arch of his eyebrow, she elaborated. "I know my parents would much sooner sleep off the effects of last night's party than go through the motions of the day with me."

"Emotional poverty." Trace echoed her statement of weeks before.

"In spades," Kate admitted tightly, swallowing against the thickness in her throat.

Trace was silent for some moments, staring moodily into the Styrofoam cup. Then, without looking up at her, he asked carefully, "Will you come back to my hotel room with me, Kate? Spend the entire day with me?"

The thickness in Kate's throat intensified. On the last day they'd spent together she'd promised him honesty and, if she were merely honest with herself, she had to acknowledge that she'd rather spend the day with him than with any other person in the world.

Observing his taut stillness, Kate knew that Trace expected her to say no. As he'd made no assurance of a "hands-off" attitude, Kate knew she should say no. But then, Kate was sick and tired of doing what she knew she should do.

"Yes, I will," she finally responded decisively.

Trace remained motionless for an instant, then he slowly raised his head to gaze at her in bemusement.

"You continually amaze me," he murmured, shaking his head slowly. "I won't hurt you, you know?"

Kate smiled tremulously. "Yes, Trace, I know."

Trace returned the smile, brightening his features—and Kate's mood. "We'll have dinner together, in my room." His eyes beginning to glow with endearing eagerness, he plucked the pastries from her lap and stuffed them into the bag. "We don't need this junk to ruin our appetites!" Gulping the last of the coffee, he dropped the cup on top of the pastries. Settling behind the wheel, he reached for the ignition key, then paused, his eyes narrowing in thought.

"And, dammit, you're going to have Christmas too!" Startling Kate with the suddenness of his action, Trace flung the car door door open. "Sit tight, kid." He grinned at her surprised expression. Sliding off the seat he strode into the store.

Staring after him in amused consternation, Kate couldn't begin to imagine why he'd gone back into the store. Five minutes later, when he pushed through the heavy glass doors, she began to laugh softly. While still moving swiftly, Trace gingerly grasped a meagerly decorated artificial tree approximately two feet tall. The scraggy thing had to be the sorriest excuse for a Christmas tree Kate had ever seen. Kate loved it on sight.

"Trace! What in the..." Kate began laughingly.

"Don't ask," Trace warned, laughing with her as he slid onto the seat and plunked the excuse in her lap. "You wouldn't believe what the manager of that store charged me for this beauty!"

"I didn't even know they sold trees in there!" Kate giggled.

"They don't." Still laughing, Trace started the engine. "It was part of their own decorations." As he drove away, he jerked his head at the store. "That guy came out ahead all the way around. Not only did I give him a ridiculous amount of money for it, now he doesn't have to clear it away after the holidays."

On their arrival at the hotel Trace coolly bore the tree through the lobby, ignoring the looks and smiles of amusement the sight drew from hotel staff and guests.

"Okay, Kate, it's your tree," Trace drawled, closing the door to his room behind them. "Where do you want it?"

Frowning, Kate glanced around the room, which was an exact duplication of the one he'd occupied the month before. "Well," she mused aloud, "if we're having dinner here we can't set it on the table by the settee. So, I suppose you'll have to put it on top of the dresser."

"Right." Grinning, Trace plopped the tree on the corner of the long dresser and plugged the one string of lights it boasted into a wall outlet. "Hmm—" he frowned, stepping back to gaze at the pitiful thing "—it needs something. Ah, I've got it!" Swinging away, he strode to the closet.

While his back was turned Kate hastily withdrew the small package from her purse and placed it under the tree before she could change her mind. Then, suddenly unsure, she walked to the window to stare blindly at the street below. Kate had to force herself to turn back to the room when Trace spoke to her.

"Come over here, Kate."

Despite the softness of his voice Kate was afraid Trace was angry about the gift. Reluctance slowing her movements, she eased around, then walked to join him at the tree.

"Look at me, Kate," Trace ordered, raising a hand to glide the tips of his fingers over her cheek. When she lifted her head, he smiled gently. "Now it looks like Christmas." With a light tug, he turned her face to the dresser.

The sight that met Kate's eyes brought a lump to her throat. There was a smaller package resting beside the one she'd placed on the dresser, its beautiful wrapping almost covered by the large bow on top. Picking the gift up, Trace held it out to her.

"Merry Christmas, Kate," he said softly.

As her hand closed on the gift, Kate held the other one out to him. "Merry Christmas, Trace."

Standing close together beside the ugly-beautiful tree, they opened the packages in unison.

"Oh, Trace!" Kate breathed in delight as she removed the lid from the box to reveal a lapel pin in the design of a shield. It was beautifully crafted in sterling silver. Emblazoned on the shield was an intricately wrought K. "How lovely! Thank you!"

"Kate! This is beautiful!" Trace exclaimed as he carefully removed the bell from its bed of tissue paper. "Thank you!"

Their voices blended as they spoke simultaneously. Then, their gazes tangling as they looked at each other, they exchanged the gift of a happy smile.

"Since we didn't get to go sightseeing last time, I brought one of the sights to you," Kate said, quickly fabricating a reason for choosing the bell.

"It's perfect," Trace murmured, caressing the glowing pewter with his fingers. "I'll keep it on my desk." A teasing light sprang into his eyes. "Have you made the connection between your gift and yourself?"

"No." Smiling back at him, Kate shook her head.

"That's the shield of honor for champions of lost little girls," he intoned. "It's only awarded to the fiercest protectors."

Kate swallowed with difficulty. "Who awards this great honor?" she asked in a whisper.

"Me." Leaning to her he brushed his lips over hers. "And I award it only once in a lifetime."

The exchanging of gifts appeared to open the lines of communication between them. Unhesitatingly, they talked the morning away and all through the light salad and wine lunch Trace ordered from room service. By the time Kate had finished her lunch and was halfway through her second glass of wine, she felt safe in asking the question uppermost in her mind.

"You said you'd tell me about love when we had the time, Trace." Kate drew a deep breath, "Do we have the time now?"

"I knew this mellow camaraderie was too good to last," Trace groaned, grimacing. Nevertheless, he answered her.

"Honey, love is an illusion. A trap." A grim smile touched his lips. "You spoke of emotional poverty. Well, love is emotional slavery. The name of love can rationalize the betrayal of previously held principles, a disregard of reasons, and even the debasement of pride." His brief burst of laughter held little humor. "I've known the illusion, Kate. From now on I'll stick to reality, and I'd advise you to do the same."

Though she wanted to cry, Kate somehow managed a weak smile. "The advice comes too late, Trace." She shrugged helplessly. "I told you that you wouldn't like hearing it."

"But that's the strange part," he murmured, looping an arm around her waist to draw her closer to his side, "I do like hearing it." Lowering his head, he inhaled the scent of her, murmuring deep in his throat when she shivered in response. "I can't offer you commitment, Kate. I won't allow myself to be emotionally enslaved again."

"I...I understand, Trace," Kate lied softly. She didn't understand, didn't *want* to understand; all she wanted was Trace!

"I don't think you do, Kate, not fully," Trace smiled. "You see, although I won't let myself *need* you emotionally, I will admit to a consuming physical need for you." His movements precise, Trace released her and sat back, giving her the opportunity to move away from him if she wished. "I enjoy your company. I can relax with you." He paused, then said distinctly, "I want to make love with you. I can't offer you more than that."

Not looking at him, Kate gave his words the consideration they deserved. Trace had complimented her with his honesty and was now allowing her the time and space she required. Within the last hours, her love for him had become an accepted absolute. Although Kate feared Trace would never change his position on love, she felt a great fear of losing him completely. Lifting her head proudly, she turned to face him.

"I want to make love with you, Trace." Kate spoke as distinctly as he had moments before. "I accept your offer."

Nine

——

Kate was on fire. Her entire body was burning. Murmuring incoherent encouragement to the man who'd ignited the blaze, she slid her fingers through the silky strands of his hair, urging him even closer to her fiery mouth. His tongue plunged in a rhythm evocative of a more intimate possession, plunged as if seeking the source of her excited murmurings.

Long spangled rays of sunlight angled through the window. It struck blue fire sparks off the black mass of Kate's hair, fanned wildly over the pillow and bathed Trace's sweat-moistened shoulders in shimmering gold. It was not the first time they'd made love that afternoon.

With Kate's acceptance of Trace's offer of a physical relationship he'd stared at her intently before slowly rising to draw her to the side of the bed. His eyes, darkened to deepest green by passion, observed the expressions washing over Kate's face as his trembling fingers slowly unfastened the buttons down the front of her shirt.

Heart pounding, barely breathing, Kate trembled with a combination of anticipation and fear of the unknown as Trace tenderly removed her clothes.

"You're a lovely woman, Kate." Trace whispered the words as he slowly ran his gaze down the length of her quivering body and back to her face. He was not touching her, yet Kate felt that gaze to the marrow of her bones; the heat of it melted the chill of fear.

Swinging her into his arms, Trace gently settled her on the bed, then stepped back to remove his own clothing. Kate watched him until his fingers began working on the waistband clip on his trousers, then she closed her eyes.

"Look at me, Kate." Though soft, his voice held a note of command. When Kate raised her eyelids the trousers were gone. Trace stood before her in navy briefs. "If we are going to be lovers there will be no barriers between us. No dishonesty, or darkness, or even closed eyes." His movements deliberate, Trace stepped out of the briefs, then straightened proudly, his sharp-eyed gaze watching for her reaction to the sight of his aroused manhood.

Kate had seen naked men before, in magazines and films, but they had not prepared her for Trace. Though magnificent in his masculine beauty, he was also rather overwhelming. Her eyes betraying the conflicting emotions tearing at her, Kate stared at him mutely.

His body taut, Trace stood absolutely still; the only part of him that moved were his lips.

"May I join you, Kate?"

Twice previously Trace had asked her permission before advancing. She knew that he would not move, either forward or back, until she answered him. Words were not needed. Kate held out her arms in silent invitation.

Trace came to her gently, but anxiously.

"I'll try not to hurt you, Kate," he said huskily, one long hand drawing shivers in it's wake as he stroked her from shoulder to hip. "But it's been so long for me, so very long, that I'm afraid...for both of us."

Even in her inexperience, Kate knew that Trace had tried to restrain himself almost past endurance. Then, his body trembling, he'd slipped between her thighs, groaning a soft whisper in her ear.

"I know you're not ready yet. Forgive me, Kate, but I must...I must."

Though most of his control was gone, still Trace initiated Kate with gentleness and caring. But, although she felt only a moment of pain and discomfort, the soaring flight of ecstasy was not hers. Yet, when Trace cried her name aloud at his own long-denied release, Kate held his shuddering body close to her own with fiercely protective possessiveness.

With Trace's face buried in the curve of her neck and his body still a part of hers, Kate lovingly stroked his relaxing form and softly denied his harsh self-condemnation.

"I shouldn't have come to you this way," he nearly growled with self-disgust. "It was grossly unfair to you."

"But better than the alternative," Kate chided softly.

Trace lifted his head to stare at her through narrowed eyelids, a smile of amusement twitching his lips. "What do you know about the alternatives?" he scoffed gently.

Kate lowered her lashes. "I know you could have...ah...*used* another woman," she said tightly. "I'm glad you didn't."

"Oh, my beautifully honest Kate!" Laughing, Trace returned his face to her neck. "What did I do to deserve you?"

"Nothing yet," Kate teased. "But, I'm hoping that you'll prove your worth very soon."

Their lovers embrace unbroken, Kate and Trace both drifted off to sleep. Kate had now awakened with the delicious feeling of being bathed by the silken stroke of Trace's tongue.

Her pale body gleaming in the afternoon sunlight, Kate arched herself into the caress of Trace's mouth and gasped his name as his teeth raked gently against her aroused nipples.

"Do you like that?" Trace murmured, repeating the action.

"Oh, yes!" Kate wasn't even certain that the purring moan was her own.

"And this?" Trace continued, trailing his fingers from her breasts to the soft flesh of her thigh.

"Yes, yes!"

"And this?" he persisted, moving his fingers in an erotic pattern. "And this," he went on relentlessly, following the path of his fingers with his hungry lips and circling tongue.

"Yes, Trace, yes!" Then, as his lips sought the honey his fingers had delicately dipped into, Kate stiffened. "Trace, no!"

His hard hands grasping her thighs, Trace raised his head to smile into her frightened eyes. "I said there'd be no barriers, Kate. There is no reason to be afraid. You are beautiful—" moving swiftly, Trace lowered his warm mouth to the heat of her "—all over."

Then, reluctantly, Trace moved away from the area of dissension, his lips leaving a moist trail of fire as he languorously made his way back to her breasts. "There are many ways to make love, darling," he murmured. "Eventually, I want to explore them all with you. I will love you in *every* way." His teeth closed gently on one sensitized nipple, eliciting a sharp gasp of pleasure from her. "And, some day, you may even want to return the compliment." Her gasp turned to a moan as he began to draw gently on her nipple.

Kate was trembling violently from the tremors quaking through her body when Trace finally kissed his way to her mouth.

"Yes," he groaned, his breathing labored. "This is the way it should be." His wine-scented breath mingled with hers. "Give me your mouth, Kate." As his lips brushed hers he moaned deeply. "I want to bury my entire body into yours."

This time Kate was more than ready for him. Burning, burning, and completely wild from the flame, she synchronized her movements to the desperate thrust of his, greedy for him. Then, her head thrown back in tension, she screamed when ecstasy caught her.

"Trace!"

"Kate!" His strained voice echoed with her name.

Exhausted, replete, Kate and Trace slept again, his arms embracing her possessively, her legs entwined with his trustingly.

"Happy birthday, Kate."

A soft "oh" sighed through Kate's lips as she came to an abrupt halt in the bathroom doorway. Her startled gaze had been caught by the flame of a single candle glowing in the dark room. The candle was set in the center of a small, frothily iced cake. Taken by surprise, Kate was oblivious to the appreciative gleam in Trace's eyes as he ran a glance over her freshly showered body. Clad in one of his shirts she appeared both vulnerable and sexy.

"Oh, Trace, thank you!" Kate exclaimed softly, looking up at him with misty eyes. "But, when—how...?"

"While you were showering," Trace replied quietly, "via room service." Walking to her, he grasped her hand to lead her to the table. "I told you I would order dinner." Dipping his head, he inhaled the scent of her still damp, freshly shampooed hair then brushed his lips over her temple. "If I had my way, you'd never wear anything but my shirts." Soft laughter rumbled in his chest. "But then, we'd probably never get out of the bedroom either."

Seating her on the settee, Trace moved the table to her. "Make a wish and blow out your candle, honey, our Christmas dinner is getting cold."

Blowing out a single candle was easy; composing a wish was even easier. With all her heart and mind, Kate wished for a softening in Trace's attitude to love and commitment.

"It's your birthday," Trace said softly, bending to kiss her lightly. "Yet I received the present. Thank you, Kate." His voice grew hoarse. "You are the most beautiful present I've ever received."

"No, Trace." Lifting her hand, Kate caressed his freshly shaven cheek. "The gift is mine. You made me a woman for my birthday." A sensuous smile curved her lips. "A very satisfied woman."

While they consumed a traditional holiday meal, Trace explained the circumstances of his return to the east coast. In turn, Kate told him of her bout with the flu. His reaction was both personal and professional. Amusement sparkling in her eyes, she calmly answered all his questions concerning her health and patiently endured his brief but thorough examination.

After the meal was finished, and they were sipping at their second cup of coffee, Kate voiced the subject uppermost in her mind.

"When are you returning to San Antonio, Trace?" Kate stared into her coffee while waiting for his answer.

"Kathy and I are booked on a flight leaving at twelve-forty tomorrow." He was quiet for several heartbeats, then he murmured, "Spend the night with me, Kate."

Kate couldn't think of anything she wanted more than sleeping curled up in his arms, but she also had responsibilities.

"I have to work tomorrow, Trace," she informed him regretfully.

"If I promise to get you home in time to get ready for work," Trace said carefully, "will you stay?"

Kate spent the night as she'd wanted, curled up in Trace's strong arms; however, she did very little sleeping.

True to his promise, Trace drove Kate home early the next morning. Pensive, quiet, they were within a few miles of her apartment before he broke the taut silence between them.

"I...I won't be able to get back to spend New Year's with you, Kate. I'm sorry, but I'll be on call for the man who's covering for me now."

Though Kate tried to hide her disappointment, she was not altogether successful. "I understand, Trace." She hesitated, then whispered, "Do you have any idea when you'll be coming east again?"

"No," he admitted tersely. "I'm sorry," he repeated.

"You needn't be." Kate glanced out the side window to conceal her tear-filled eyes. "You've made no promises."

"Come with me, Kate." There was a sudden urgency in his tone. For one tiny instant, hope flared wildly in Kate; it died painfully with his next words. "Let me take an apartment for you in San Antonio. Let me take care of you."

Kate's head was moving back and forth before he'd finished speaking. "No, Trace. I want to be with you," she confessed, "but not like that."

The sigh that escaped his lips revealed Trace's frustration. "I want to ask you to promise me that you won't see any other man, or *be* with any other man, but I won't." Trace expelled his breath harshly. "I know I don't have any right to ask that of you, Kate."

"I've already granted you the right, Trace." Turning to him, Kate smiled, if sadly. "I don't want to see or *be* with any other man. I love you, Trace. I'll be here for you, always, whether you want me or not."

At that moment, Trace pulled the car along the curb in front of her apartment. After switching off the ignition, he turned to her, a self-derisive smile twisting his lips.

"Oh, I want you, Kate." Reaching out, he dragged her across the seat, crushing her slim body to his. "God, how I want you!"

Trace held her trembling body protectively, compulsively for a long time, murmuring endearments and instructions alternately.

"Take care of yourself, sweetheart."

"I will," Kate whispered.

"Don't forget to take your vitamins, honey."

"I won't," she promised.

"Get plenty of rest, don't overdo, baby."

"I'll try," she laughed, sobbingly.

"I'll call you, love."

"I'll be here."

After parking the car in front of the narrow town-house of his former in-laws, Trace rested his head for an instant on the cold steering wheel. How was it possible, he wondered miserably. He'd left Kate at the door to her apartment less than half an hour before, yet already he was missing her to the point of near pain!

Feeling raw, his mouth set in a grimly forbidding line, Trace stepped from the car, mounted the three marble steps to the front door and rang the bell with an impatient jab of his finger. Ruth Parker met him in the narrow, elegant foyer.

"Kathy will be down in a moment, Trace," Ruth smiled in genuine welcome. "Won't you come in and sit down?"

"No, thank you, Ruth," Trace responded tersely. "I have something to say, and I prefer to say it here."

"What is it, Trace?" Ruth asked apprehensively.

Trace didn't hesitate. "You do realize that if Annette persists in going ahead with this lawsuit, I can't bring Kathy east anymore?" he stated unequivocally.

"But, Trace!" Ruth cried. "Kathy's so very young! She'll forget me and her grandfather!"

"Yes, she will," Trace acknowledged stonily. "And I'll be sorry for that. But I can't afford to take chances." His expression settled into unrelenting lines. "Regardless of how a Pennsylvania judge rules, I am not giving Kathy up. If I must, I'll barricade my home and hire a twenty-four-hour guard around it."

Ruth's still lovely face seemed to crumble before his eyes, leaving her looking old and afraid. "Oh, Trace, I know what Annette is doing is wrong! I've talked to her...we've all talked to her, even Carl and Barbara, but she refuses to listen to reason.''

Trace hid the surprise he felt at learning that Annette's older sister Barbara had championed his cause; personally, he'd always considered his former sister-in-law even more self-centered than Annette. Casting speculation about the motives of Annette's sister aside, Trace said dryly, ''Maybe you've all been talking to the wrong person.'' When Ruth frowned in confusion, he clarified, ''Perhaps you should talk to Randall—'' he drawled the name sarcastically ''—he's the one pressuring Annette to bring the suit.''

Ruth's astonished expression convinced Trace she'd known nothing of Randall's part in Annette's scheme. Instinct assured Trace that before long Randall was going to find himself face-to-face with two outraged grandparents. The smile that curved Trace's lips was not pleasant.

''If you do talk to him,'' he went on softly. ''You can give him a message from me. Tell *Randall* that I said there's absolutely *no* way he'll get my daughter.''

The fact that Kathy was unnaturally subdued didn't dawn on Trace until after they'd arrived home. Distracted by memories of the hours he'd spent with Kate, his daughter's odd behavior didn't hit him until she'd finished opening the Christmas presents waiting at home for her. It was her unenthusiastic reception that finally pierced Trace's absorbed thoughts.

''What's the matter, honey?'' Trace frowned. ''Don't you like what Santa brought you?''

''Yes, I guess so,'' Kathy mumbled, sniffing. ''But he didn't bring me the only thing I asked for and really, really wanted.''

Drawing her into his arms, Trace murmured. "But what *did* you ask him for, Kath?" With a gentle finger, he wiped the first of the tears from her soft cheek.

"I asked Santa if I could have Kate for my mommie for Christmas," Kathy sobbed pitifully.

Closing his eyes, Trace laid his cheek against Kathy's shining blond hair. Why not? he quizzed himself, aching all over for the sight of Kate, the sound of her, the feel of her beneath him. Then, coming to his senses, Trace grimaced at his own weakness and chastened his daughter gently.

"I suppose this was as good a time as any for you to learn that we simply can't have everything we want, Kath."

For Kate, life became encapsulated within the intervals Trace could manage to fly east to spend a day or two with her; the rest of her time was mere existence. And those intervals didn't happen very often.

She spent New Year's Eve sitting by the phone, willing it to ring. Trace called exactly one minute after twelve.

"Happy New Year, honey," he greeted her softly. "What were you doing?"

"Watching the ball descend in Times Square and praying you would call," Kate replied with artless honesty.

"Oh, Kate!" Though Trace laughed, it sounded forced and rueful. "You don't know the meaning of the word guile, do you?"

"Oh, yes, I know the meaning," Kate responded steadily. "I just don't see the point in using it. You know how I feel, nothing I say or do will change that."

There were times over the months that followed when Kate wished with all her might that she could somehow fall out of love with Trace. There were times when she'd counted the reasons why she should break it off with him, refuse to see him on the rare occasions he found he could spare the time to see her. But those times were immediately forgotten when he showed up at her apartment, pulling her into his arms the minute she opened the door.

And, when they were together, the only thought in Kate's mind was how very much she loved him.

They had one glorious weekend together in January. The instant Trace arrived, Kate looked at him and knew something had occurred to ease the lines of strain on his face. At her careful questioning, Trace smiled with relief and satisfaction.

"I had a call from Ruth Parker yesterday," he explained, his smile growing into a grin. "Annette got married in Paris on Thursday." His laughter had a young sound. "Since Ruth, her husband *and* her son and daughter all apparently had a hand in convincing Annette's new husband of the futility of a custody suit, I could almost feel sorry for him."

As if infused with new life and purpose, Trace was tireless throughout that weekend. Laughing with the emotional high he was on, he swung her into his arms and carried her to the bedroom.

"What do you think you're doing?" Kate gasped with a startled burst of laughter.

"I want to celebrate." Trace paused in the doorway to her bedroom to gaze at her with eyes greenly opaque with desire. "And, my sweet, the best way I can think of to celebrate is by making love to you until you beg me to make you mine."

Kate's chest grew tight from a sudden lack of oxygen. Her breathing sporadic and almost painful, she curled her arms around his taut neck and brushed her parted lips over his warm skin. The musky-spicy scent of him sent her senses whirling out of control.

"I can't wait," she confessed throatily, stabbing the tip of her tongue into the hollow behind his ear.

"Where did you learn to do that?" Trace groaned, tightening his grip to crush her to the unyielding hardness of his chest.

"Don't you like it?" Kate almost purred, gliding her tongue around the outer curl of his ear.

"Like it!" Trace growled, nipping at her cheek. "Honey, I *love* it!" Entering the room he closed the door with one sharp, backward kick of his booted foot. "And now," he murmured in a deep, dark, sexy voice, "I'm going to love you."

Kate's pulse accelerated into overdrive as Trace slid her to her feet. Her breathing grew shallow as he began to undress her with trembling fingers. When, finally, she stood before him as nature had fashioned her, she shivered from the heat of the fiery gaze. Without conscious direction her hands lifted to his chest and she was brushing the heavy jacket off of his shoulders.

Trace didn't help Kate in her unaccustomed role of valet. Inept though her fingers were, she managed to remove every article of clothing he was wearing. Trace's flanks quivered as she knelt to glide his navy-blue briefs to his ankles and off his feet.

"You did promise me that you were a faster learner," he said unevenly, raspily, as he bent to grasp her shoulders to draw her up to him.

Kate resisted his effort and, clasping him around the waist, fastened her moist lips to his flat abdomen.

"Oh, Kate!" Trace's voice was rough with the need coursing through him. "What are you trying to do?"

"Learn," Kate mumbled, touching him with the tip of her tongue. "Does this please you, Trace?" Once more her tongue flicked out to inflict exquisite sensations on his body.

"Please me! Sweet Lord, love! It drives me crazy!" Trace was now breathing with obvious difficulty. "Oh, Kate!" he moaned when her tongue stroked his sensitive skin. "You don't have to do this, darling." Even as he spoke his body shuddered with pleasure.

"But I want to, I want to help you celebrate," Kate whispered an instant before she tasted him.

Their celebration was an unqualified success.

Trace didn't check into a hotel that weekend. Upon awakening from the nap that had followed their wildly enthusiastic lovemaking, he retrieved his valise from the rented car and dropped it at the foot of the bed where Kate was still sleepily ensconced.

"I'm not letting you out of my sight this weekend," he said adamantly, eyeing her warily as if expecting an argument.

"Good," Kate murmured mildly, smothering a yawn with her hand. Smiling inwardly she watched surprise widen Trace's eyes, and wondered exactly what kind of relationship he'd had with his ex-wife. Aching for the man inside the wall he'd built around himself, Kate slid her body into a sitting position and allowed the smile to reach her kiss-swollen lips. "Were you planning to feed me?" Before he could respond, she chided, "I really must have fortification if you intend to indulge in more bedroom gymnastics."

"Kate, you're fantastic!" Trace's warm laughter flowed over her an instant before his body came crashing onto the bed beside her.

"Trace!" she yelped, giggling as he caught her to him in a fierce bear hug.

"Kate!" he mimicked, sinking his teeth gently into her shoulder. "I definitely will feed you, honey," he growled, working his teeth against the curve of her neck. "But, for myself, I think I'll have you for dinner." Trace proceeded to demonstrate his meaning in the most delightful way possible.

Long, wonderful hours later, after a sumptuous dinner in the most expensive restaurant Kate could think of and followed by dreamy hours held molded to Trace's body while dancing, Kate lay wakeful beside her contentedly sleeping lover.

What sort of relationship *had* Trace had with his wife? The nagging question was the thief robbing Kate of sleep. From their first, glorious loving on his arrival, Trace had appeared to shrug off care like a weight that had been dragging him down. Set free, he was a charming companion, a thrilling lover, a good friend. Yet Kate sensed that he still retained a part of himself. Her fear was that Trace would always retain a part of himself.

Choking bitterness rose in Kate's throat against the woman who had hurt Trace so badly that he was determined never to leave himself open to another woman. For while he had spoken passionately of loving, his words had concerned the physical, not the emotional kind.

Acceptance was a bitter pill but, once swallowed, Kate gently drifted into slumber; she would take whatever Trace offered. She had no choice, she loved him.

In February Trace sent Kate an enormous heart-shaped, elegantly decorated box of chocolates. When she saw the manufacturer's name inscribed discreetly on the bottom of the box, Kate gasped aloud; the gift had to have cost Trace the better part of a hundred dollars. But, though he called at least three times a week, Trace could not arrange to fly east during the entire month.

On the second Friday in March, Trace called Kate at the office to ask if she could pick him up at the airport that evening. Excited, so eager to see him that she could barely sit at her desk the remainder of the afternoon, Kate agonized through the hours until she saw his beloved face as he strode off the covered ramp and into the waiting lounge. Unconscious of the milling people around her, Kate launched herself into his arms and fastened her mouth on his.

"I've missed you, Kate," Trace groaned close to her ear.

"And I've missed you," Kate choked, fighting tears.

And so it went on. Trace managed an overnight stay the last week in March, and an entire three days in mid-April. While they were together they made love often, sometimes with such passionate abandonment it bordered on the violent.

In truth, it was the desperate quality of their lovemaking that initiated the first curls of unease in Kate's mind.

How long could a love affair survive when the lovers were separated by half a continent? Although Kate tried to avoid recognizing the niggling unease, once the question was in her mind, it refused to be dislodged or ignored.

By steeping herself in her love for Trace, Kate had literally withdrawn from her friends, both male and female. Could she continue to function healthily when she was really only fully alive while she was with Trace?

Trace, on the other hand, was apparently having no difficulty whatever with their less than normal situation. He laughed often, loved ardently, and even spoke freely of his work and home life for the first time.

"Kath talks about you incessantly to Inez."

The information came out of the blue while they strolled along Penn's Landing in the warmth of the April sunshine.

"Inez?" Kate frowned; who the devil was this Inez?

"My housekeeper." The way Trace answered, it was obvious he assumed Kate knew the woman's identity. Then he frowned. "I've mentioned her before—haven't I?"

"No." Kate shook her head. "Is...ah...is she pretty?" She hadn't wanted to ask, yet she couldn't prevent the words from spilling out of her jealous mouth.

"Inez?" Trace shot her a look of amazement. He opened his mouth, then closed it again, an unholy gleam dancing in his eyes. "Ravishing," he said fervently, "and she sleeps in, you know." His smile was devilish.

Kate was being had, she knew she was being had, yet she was powerless against the question, or the frigid tone that coated her voice.

"With you?"

"Oh, my precious Kate!" Laughing delightedly, Trace hauled her into his arms with supreme disregard for any onlookers. "Were you afraid that, having given up the vow of abstinence, I was indulging my libido with every available female?"

Kate sniffed disdainfully. Trace kissed her hard on the mouth.

"Inez is a lovely woman," he murmured into her ear. "She is also in her sixties." His arms tightened around her possessively. "*You* are the only woman I sleep with. The only woman I want to sleep with." Loosening his embrace, he leaned back to stare directly into her eyes. "You satisfy all my wants, Kate."

"And you mine," Kate sighed, feeling ridiculously happy.

While they were together Kate was content. It was during the long periods of separation that she grew restless, uneasily questioning the wisdom of indulging herself and her love.

In early May Trace flew east again, but this time their reunion was different; this time Trace brought Kathy with him.

"Kate!" Kathy's squeal and the way her little face became suddenly animated brought a tight feeling to Kate's throat and chest.

Stooping down, Kate held her arms open to the child. Tears running down her face, Kathy flew into Kate's welcoming embrace.

"Oh, Kate! I hoped and hoped I'd see you," Kathy chattered happily. "But I was afraid daddy wouldn't let me!"

Hugging the child, Kate raised her eyes to Trace, who mouthed the words, "I missed you." Kate didn't reply, but then, she didn't need to, her eyes told him of her heartfelt joy at seeing him.

The two-day visit was an unqualified success. Though there was no time or opportunity for any physical activity of the bedroom variety, Kathy gave Kate and Trace plenty of physical activity of the sightseeing type. Her little body practically quivering with excitement, Kathy insisted on viewing everything Philadelphia had to offer the tourist.

By the time Kate saw Trace and Kathy off at the airport, her affections were secured within the child's tiny hand. At the same time, Kate was also well versed on the many attractions of San Antonio. Brimming with enthusiasm and the wistfully voiced hope that Kate would visit her one day, Kathy sang the praises of the Alamo, the famous walk along the San Antonio River, the Mexican Market—El Mercado, the Spanish Governor's Palace, the Tower of the Americas—or as Kathy described it, "the needle-shaped thing with a restaurant on top"—and King William Street with it's beautifully restored Victorian homes.

Though Kate laughingly told Kathy she'd love to see all the sights the girl had described, in her heart Kate knew the one sight she longed to see was Trace, welcoming her to his home city and his life.

By mid-July, both Kate and Trace were showing signs of the strain inflicted by their unorthodox relationship. Trace "stole" three whole days away from his overloaded schedule that week. Using Kate's car they drove to a small, quiet resort town along the New Jersey coast. They spent the entire three days laying on the beach basking in the sun during the day, and laying on the bed basking in each other most of the night.

In early August Trace made an overnight, surprise visit. Only Trace got the surprise.

Hot and irritable, Kate opened the door for Trace with a scowl and stepped back to avoid his arms.

Eyeing her warily, Trace followed Kate into the stuffy living room, shedding his lightweight summer suit jacket as he walked.

"Don't you have air-conditioning in here?" he asked, undoing the top three buttons on his shirt. "This place is an oven."

"Yes, I have air-conditioning," Kate snapped. "The damned thing died this morning."

Trace threw her a startled look; Kate rarely swore. "Have you called a repairman?" he inquired carefully.

"No, I can't afford it until I get paid next week," Kate turned away impatiently.

"Oh, for heaven's sake!" Trace exclaimed. "If you needed money, why didn't you call me?" As he was pacing the room, Trace missed the spark of anger that flared in Kate's eyes. "Go freshen up, honey, and we'll go shopping. I'll buy you a new air-conditioner."

"No, Trace."

Though her tone was soft, Trace couldn't miss the anger lacing her voice. "Why not?" he frowned. "You'll suffocate in here."

"I don't want you to buy things for me, Trace," Kate said adamantly.

His smile coaxing, Trace walked to her. Raising his hand, he caressed her perspiration-wet face with his fingers. "Why not, honey?" he asked softly. "I would enjoy buying you anything you wanted."

Kate's lips tightened. "And what would accepting your gifts make me?" Kate smiled mirthlessly. "There are several names that come to mind. Mistress is among them."

"Kate!" Trace barked, grasping her by the shoulders. "What are you saying? Do you know?" He pulled her into his arms with angry strength. "I never think about you in that way, and you know it," he said roughly.

"Do I?" Shrugging out of his arms, Kate clasped her arms around herself as if she were freezing in the stifling room. "I still don't want you to buy me gifts."

Trace exhaled raggedly. "All right." Turning toward the small kitchen, he sighed. "Do you have any tools? I'll see if I can get it running. We can't sleep in his oven."

At his last statement, something that had been slowly building over the last few weeks finally broke through. Swinging around, she ridiculed, "You're a surgeon, Trace, not an appliance repairman. And, if you're afraid of losing sleep, sleep somewhere else."

"Kate..." Trace began in obvious confusion that had a thread of impatient anger.

"As a matter of fact," she cut him off, "why don't you go back to San Antonio. Visit the Alamo. Take a walk by the river. Operate on someone!"

"Maybe I will," Trace snarled, grabbing his jacket from the chair as he strode to the door.

"Trace!"

Trace paused with his hand on the doorknob. "What?"

"Don't come back." Kate stared into his astonished eyes. What was she doing? Why was she doing it, she demanded of herself as she stiffened her spine. Kate knew why, had known it for weeks. She just hadn't wanted to admit to the growing sense of despair that engulfed her every time Trace left her, or face the utter hopelessness she endured after he was gone.

"Kate, honey, what are you saying?" Releasing his hold on the knob, Trace moved to her. "You don't mean it."

"I do, Trace." And in that instant, Kate realized that she did. She loved him so very much. Perhaps too much, because she knew inside that the day was swiftly approaching when watching him walk away from her would kill her soul—if it hadn't already.

"I won't be here for you anymore, Trace."

Trace came to a stop inches from her, his eyes as hard and flat as unpolished gemstones. "I see." His lips curled cynically. "It was a short-lived illusion—wasn't it, Kate?"

Kate opened her mouth to deny his assertion. All that came out was a gasped "oh" as Trace hauled her roughly against him and crushed her lips to his. The kiss was brief and very close to brutal. Releasing her as swiftly as he'd grabbed her, Trace pivoted and strode to the door, yanking it open violently. Before crossing the threshold he paused to glance back at her.

"I can't say I'm surprised because I'm not," he said tiredly. "The surprising thing is that I know I'm going to miss you like hell."

The slam of the door punctuated his admission.

"Trace." Kate's cry was little more than a whimper of anguish; Trace didn't hear it; Kate hadn't meant him to.

Exactly how long she stood, unmoving, staring at nothing, Kate had no idea, nor was she aware of the ache of tension in her taut muscles. All Kate was aware of was the growing emptiness inside, yawning wider and wider, threatening to swallow her up in a black void.

By morning she was not only uncomfortably hot and emotionally drained, but she had a severe headache as well. When her doorbell rang just after noon, Kate answered it frowningly. The way things were running, she thought cynically, it was probably her mother.

"Miss Warren?" The man at her door was wearing a shirt with the name of a local florist stitched on the breast pocket, and he was holding a tissue-wrapped bouquet in his hand. At Kate's nod, he handed the bouquet to her. "These are for you, miss."

"Thank you." Kate accepted the bouquet with a sensation of déjà vu. The difference was, this time she knew the flowers were not from Trace.

Kate was wrong. After tipping the delivery man, she carried the bouquet to the sofa and placed it on the coffee table exactly as she had at Christmas time. Still frowning, she slid the tiny card from its envelope. There were three words scrawled across the card in Trace's now familiar penmanship. Three words that brought a gasp to her lips and a flood of tears to her eyes.

Marry me, Kate.

Kate was staring at the blurred message when the doorbell rang again. Tugging a tissue from the box on the table at the end of the sofa, Kate blotted the tears on her cheeks as she went to the door.

"May I come in?"

Kate's stomach muscles contracted. Dressed in western-style, slim-leg jeans and a short-sleeved cotton knit pullover, Trace was the most appealing man she'd ever seen. His naturally unruly hair was mussed, as if he'd been raking impatient fingers through the deep waves. There were dark smudges beneath his somber green eyes. Deep grooves scored his face from the outer edge of his nostrils to the corners of his mouth. He looked tired and dispirited, and Kate might have given in to the need to fling herself into his arms...if that now detested, cynical twist had disappeared from his lips—but it hadn't, and she didn't.

Not answering verbally, Kate turned away and walked back into the room, leaving the door standing wide open.

A fatalistic shudder swayed her rigidly held body at the sound of the door closing quietly.

Kate didn't hear Trace move, yet she knew he was standing very close to her. Her senses quivered with the scent and feel of him. Without conscious thought her eyes sought the little card she still clutched in her hand. Trace didn't miss the slight movement of her fingers as they tightened on the note.

"Well, will you?" he asked in a harsh raspy tone.

Kate didn't need time to think; she knew what her answer had to be. "No, Trace, I won't marry you." Kate's nails slashed her palms; knowing what she had to say was one thing, saying it was quite another. When Trace sighed she felt it in her throat.

"Can't you even look at me, Kate?"

Molding her features into an unemotional mask, Kate turned to face him. She immediately wished she hadn't moved. Trace looked angry, frustrated, and even more cynical than before.

"Why not?" Trace unconsciously echoed his query of seven months previously. "We get along well," he smiled that hateful smile. "At least we have up until now. You're obviously fond of Kathy." He smiled again. "We're dynamite together in bed. We could make it work." He drew a deep breath, then added, as if it were an added attraction, "I'd give you anything you wanted, Kate."

Kate smiled in a cynical parody of his. "No, Trace, we couldn't make it work. A month ago, two weeks ago, possibly even three days ago, I'd have said yes without giving my answer any consideration at all."

"Then why..." Trace exploded.

"Because now, today, I realize how wrong it would be," Kate interrupted him calmly. "Don't you see, Trace? None of the reasons you've given me are enough.

I thought I could do it." Kate swallowed against the thickness in her throat. "I loved you so much, wanted you so much that I really thought I could be satisfied with what you offered me." Kate smiled sadly. "Now I find I'm greedy. I want it all, Trace. And, if I can't have it all, I don't want any of it."

Ten

────────

It was after midnight, and it was still very hot and very humid. His movements almost stealthy, Trace let himself into the house by the back door. The only sounds in the quiet night were the muffled click of the lock and the faint rattle of the chain being engaged.

Moving silently through the dark hallway, Trace entered his office, shutting the door before flicking the light on. Crossing directly to the credenza, he splashed a double measure of whiskey into a heavy, squat glass and sank wearily into his desk chair.

Raising the glass, he drank deeply, expelling his breath with a soft whoosh as the liquor left a trail of fire down his throat. The moment he'd tossed back the last swallow of whiskey he got up to refill his glass again.

Why not, he mused wryly. He was on vacation, wasn't he? He could look forward to two whole weeks without a waiting room overflowing with patients or back-to-back operations to perform. Two whole weeks! Trace smiled bitterly.

After nearly a month of maintaining a schedule designed to fill as many minutes as possible in every sixteen-hour day, Trace was bone tired. All he'd needed on the Friday before Labor Day, and his last working day before starting his vacation, was trouble in the operating room. So, naturally, that was exactly what he'd gotten.

Shuddering, Trace relived the moment his anesthetist said, tersely, "The patient's heart has stopped beating, doctor!"

Twelve hours! Trace shuddered again. For twelve hours his own team plus a specialized heart team had worked to revive the patient. They'd succeeded too! Trace felt both gratitude and pride for the heart specialists and his own hand-picked team.

What a way to begin a vacation, Trace grimaced. He'd been straddling the fine edge of exhaustion before he'd walked into the operating room that morning. Then he'd spent twelve hours fighting death on its own ground. Trace didn't feel victorious. He felt drained.

Setting his glass aside, Trace propped his elbows on the desk top and dropped his face in his hands, massaging his eyes and temples with his fingertips. As he raised his head his gaze came to rest on the pewter replica of the Liberty Bell. Lowering his right hand, he stroked the smooth metal.

It hadn't worked. All the countless hours of driving himself to the point of numbness hadn't dulled the tearing pain.

Kate.

Trace grasped the little bell and brought it to his face, rubbing it absently against the taut skin on his cheek. Closing his eyes, he conjured an image of her, her smoky-gray eyes darkened to near black with the passion he'd aroused in her, her pale skin gleaming slickly in the aftermath of that passion. Her beautiful mouth pressed to the pulse throbbing in his throat.

Scenes of the moments they'd shared flickered in his mind like a reel of film on a projector gone haywire: Kate, bristling at him on the day they met; Kate, gazing at him, solemn-eyed and trusting the very next day in his hotel room; Kate, giving herself to him in sweet abandonment on Christmas Day—her birthday; Kate, laughing with Kathy as she answered each and every one of the child's endless questions the day they'd finally gone sightseeing; and Kate, her eyes betraying anguish, her voice sad on the day he'd asked her to marry him.

What if it had been Kate on the operating table that day? Trace thought in sudden terror. And what if he or some other surgeon lost the battle against death?

"No!"

Trace sprang to his feet as the denial exploded from his throat. He couldn't lose Kate! He wouldn't! Not to death, if he could prevent it. And certainly not to his blasted pride!

A rush of adrenaline generated energy through his body as Trace strode from the office up to his bedroom. Refreshed by a stinging hot-cold shower, he threw clothes into his carryon with little concern for neatness. Then, dressed in a summer suit, he carried the case to the window in his office that faced east. Motionless, Trace watched the horizon for the first pink streaks of dawn.

Would the nightmare never end? Would the pain never subside? Pacing a well-worn path from the kitchen to the living-room window, Kate gazed at the wilting signs of summer's demise. The tiny patch of lawn that fronted the house was withered in spots. The trees that lined the sidewalk drooped, the leaves were drained of life.

It was Saturday of a holiday weekend. Her eyes as lifeless as the leaves she stared at, Kate grimaced with memory. She had met Trace on a Saturday of a holiday weekend. After the grinding weeks she'd just struggled through, Kate felt positive she would hate holiday weekends until the day she died.

Determined not to sink into gloom, Kate retraced her steps to the kitchen. She'd been up for hours, yet she hadn't eaten a thing. Food. That was the answer, Kate assured herself for at least the thousandth time over the previous weeks. Food was the best tranquilizer for emotional upset, especially chocolate.

Fifteen minutes later, a steaming cup of coffee cradled in her hands, Kate regarded the chocolate-filled croissant on a plate in front of her with emotional hunger.

By feeding that hunger, Kate had gained seven pounds over the last four weeks. The food had failed to appease the starvation. Breaking a corner off the flaky croissant, she gazed at it unenthusiastically before dropping it back onto the plate.

No, Kate protested silently. She didn't want food, she wanted Trace.

Trace.

The coffee forgotten, Kate closed her eyes, filling her mind with an image of him. What was he doing, now, this minute? It was Saturday so he was probably not in his office. Was he applying his skill in the operating room? Or, as this was a holiday weekend, was he free for a few days? It was an hour earlier in San Antonio. Was he still asleep? Did he ever dream of her?

Raising the cup to her lips, Kate gulped back a sob along with the tepid brew. Would the nightmare of memories never end? Would the pain of remembrance never subside?

Glancing at the clock, Kate told herself to get cracking. She had made a date to go shopping with Lisa, the girl who sat next to her at the office.

While showering, then dressing in a denim skirt, sleeveless blouse and flat sandals, Kate asked herself why she'd ever agreed to the shopping expedition in the first place. As she applied blusher to her pale cheeks, she answered her own question. She'd holed-up inside her apartment far too long. She had to get out, be with people, laugh with someone if she ever hoped to forget each and every moment she'd spent with Trace.

The shopping trip was a complete failure. Though Kate talked animatedly with Lisa, the words were meaningless. Though she laughed often, the laughter was hollow. When she and Lisa stopped for lunch, Kate picked at her food, but drank two margaritas thirstily. When she began to feel maudlin, Kate sagely advised herself to go home.

Trace was waiting for Kate in the hallway. The sight of his lean body propped lazily against the doorframe brought Kate to a dead stop as she rounded the corner into the hall at the top of the stairs. His haggard expression caused a contraction in her chest that robbed her of breath. But even with the look of a man honed to a cutting edge, he was the most attractive male Kate had seen in weeks...four weeks.

"I must talk to you, Kate." Straightening tautly, Trace ran a devouring glance over her, his shadowed eyes revealing stark hunger when they came to a stop on her trembling lips.

Suddenly hot, and cold, and exceedingly nervous, Kate slicked her tongue over her parched lips, swallowing roughly when his eyes narrowed at her unconsciously sensuous action.

"I...ah...all right." Forcing her tongue and feet to move at the same time, Kate closed the distance between them. Her fingers shook uncontrollably as she inserted the door key into the lock. Kate's entire body jerked when his long fingers covered hers to guide the key into the slot. When he removed his hand to push the door open, she rushed into the room, stiffening with tension when door shut quietly behind them.

Not looking at him, afraid to look at him, Kate dumped her impulsively bought, not really wanted, purchases on the sofa. Turning slowly, she drew a deep breath. "Would you—" she paused to swallow "—would you like something to drink?" Without waiting for his response, she started for the kitchen.

"No, Kate, I don't want anything to drink." The rough edge on Trace's tone brought her to a quivering halt. The quiver intensified as he continued, "I said I must talk to you. Please look at me while I say what I have to say."

Distractedly shaking her head, she changed course, moving toward the bedroom. Kate was not consciously aware of either action. She was in retreat. Positive Trace was about to plead with her to resume their relationship, and uncertain of her strength of will or her ability to refuse him, she ran into the bedroom. Trace was right behind her.

"Kate!" Without pause, Trace crossed the room to her. "Will you please just listen to me?"

Her breathing erratic, her heartbeat thundering, every one of her senses drinking in the scent of him, the nearness of him, Kate gritted her teeth against the desire to turn and throw herself into his arms. When he got to within inches of her, she ran into the bathroom, locking the door with shaking fingers.

"Kate." Though muffled, his low groan seeped into the room to stab at her heart.

Leaning forward, Trace rested his forehead on the smooth wood that separated them. Had he waited too long? Trace lowered his blunt lashes against the unfamiliar sting of tears in his eyes. Dear God! Had he indulged his pride to the point of losing her?

"Kate?" Trace made no attempt to conceal the pain in his voice; he was past subterfuge. "Kate, can you hear me?" There was a long moment of quiet, during which Trace held his breath.

"Yes, Trace," she finally responded, unwillingly.

"Kate, please open the door." Trace was oblivious to the hot trickle of moisture that ran down his face. "I have to look at you. I have to hold you. Kate, I need you!"

Stunned into immobility, Kate slowly closed her eyes. Had she actually heard Trace Sinclair user the word need? A sob rose in her constricted throat. Oh, please, please make it true! Suddenly frantic with the need to witness that truth, Kate fumbled in her haste to unlock the door. Flinging it open, she searched his eyes through a misty veil of tears. Her own eyes widened in sheer disbelief at the evidence of tears on his cheeks and lashes. But more astounding still was the pain revealed unashamedly in those green depths.

"Trace?" Kate's tone held awed wonder.

Though his burning gaze clung to hers, Trace made no move to touch her. "I love you, Kate. I need you." The steady tenor of his voice banished all shreds of doubt in Kate's heart and mind. "I need you in my home. I need you in my bed. I need you in my life." He paused, then smiled tentatively. "Come to Texas with me, Kate."

"Oh, Trace!" Kate was now sobbing; her defenses dissolving in a flood of healing tears. "I love you so much, Trace," she whispered. "So very much."

His smile tender, Trace held out his arms. "Come to me, my love." Gathering her body close to the protective warmth of his own, Trace lowered his lips to her hair. Holding her tightly, he absorbed her tremors with his own.

Blond curls dancing on her shoulders, the little girl skipped along happily between the adults that flanked her on either side. As they exited the brightly decorated department store she raised her hands to grasp the two that were extended to her. The early evening air was balmy on the expectant face she lifted to the man.

"Can we eat dinner in town, daddy?" Kathy requested hopefully.

Trace smiled down at his daughter before exchanging a glance with his wife. "What do you think, Kate?" he inquired blandly, his green eyes teasing. "Did this little imp behave herself while you were finishing your shopping? Has she earned dinner in town?''

Gazing down at her stepdaughter, Kate winked conspiratorially; they'd had a delightful day, shopping for Trace's Christmas present. "Yes," Kate nodded decisively. "In fact, she not only behaved nicely, she was a great deal of help. Kathy has not only earned the right to dinner in town, she's earned the privilege of choosing the restaurant."

"Okay, honey, the choice is yours. Where would you like to eat?" Trace grinned. "But let me warn you, if you choose a pizza parlor you're in big trouble."

Kathy grinned back at him. "I want to eat along the river walk so I can look at the lights."

"Mexican?" Trace asked with almost boyish expectancy.

"Of course!" Kathy and Kate laughed as their answering voices blended in unison.

Sitting at an umbrella-shaded table on the lower level of the restaurant's tiered patio, Kate was lulled by the gentle lap of the San Antonio River as it slapped the cement siding walls. Her gray eyes reflecting the enchantment shining from Kathy's face, Kate gazed up at the tall trees lining the river walk. Still in full leaf, the trees were ablaze with lights strung through their branches.

Incredible, thought Kate, smiling as a boatload of tourists waved at the diners as the boat glided by. Back east she, and most of those tourists, would be huddling inside heavy winter wear. While here in San Antonio they were all attired in lightweight clothing. Incredible.

Breathing in the warm, scented air, Kate lifted her glass to sip the tangy margarita she'd ordered. Even the drinks taste better here, she thought, smiling at Trace over the rim of her glass. Or, she mused, was it being with Trace that made the air seem warmer, the Christmas lights brighter, the drink tangier?

"Have you decided?"

Kate blinked herself out of her reverie and into the reality of softly shaded green eyes smiling into hers. "Hmm?" she murmured vaguely, admiring the way his unruly chestnut hair persisted in falling onto his forehead.

"I asked if you have decided what you'd like for dinner." Trace smiled in acknowledgment of her caressing gaze. "The waitress is waiting." Turning his head slightly, he smiled at the patient young Mexican-American.

"Oh!" Kate shifted her apologetic glance to the waitress. "Yes, I'm sorry!"

The young woman smiled in understanding. "It is comforting to gaze out over the river. There is no rush here, *señora*."

Señora. Kate very much liked the sound of the word; it was what Inez called her. After ordering, Kate turned her attention to Kathy.

"The lights are beautiful. Aren't they?"

"Oh, yes!" Kathy sighed, looking up at the trees.

"As beautiful as that huge tree you fell in love with in that shopping mall last year?" Trace teased softly.

"Yes," Kathy nodded emphatically. "That tree was beautiful too, but in a different way."

"And the Santa Claus you whispered to before we left the store, was he as nice as the one you talked to last year?" Trace drawled, arching his eyebrows.

Kate frowned. Though she was positive his question had a definite purpose, she couldn't begin to imagine what it might be.

With the innocence of the very young, Kathy went right to the heart of the matter. "Yes, he was nice. Why?"

Trace shrugged. "I was wondering if you were planning to tell us what you asked him to bring you, or if it is a deep, dark secret like last year."

Now Kate was really confused; what was Kathy's secret last year? Trace answered her question before she could voice it.

"Kathy asked Santa for you to be her mommie last year, Kate."

"Oh, Kathy!" Tears welling in her eyes, Kate reached across the table to grasp the child's hand. "Did you really want me for your mommie, baby?"

"Yes." Kathy nodded shyly. "But Santa didn't bring you. I cried and cried."

"And are there going to be any tears this year?" Trace probed gently.

"No." Kathy set her curls dancing with a quick shake of her head. "I don't think so. I only asked Santa for two things."

Holding the girl's hand, Kate waited for Kathy to elaborate; Trace displayed far less patience.

"Well?" he nudged exasperatedly.

Kathy gazed up at him with wide, trusting eyes. "I asked for a Barbie dollhouse," she said simply, then, very quickly, "and a baby brother."

Kate's eyes flashed to Trace even as his gaze shot to hers. There was an instant of silence, then they both burst out laughing.

"Did I ask for the wrong thing again?" Kathy wailed plaintively.

"No!" Trace choked trying to subdue a fresh peel of laughter.

"Of course not!" Kate soothed, stroking the confused child's hand. "But, honey, I hope you realize that Santa can't bring you a baby brother *or* sister *this* year?"

Kathy's lower lip protruded in a pout. "Why?"

"Well...because..." Kate floundered. How in the world did one explain the time element involved in procreation to a four-year-old?

"Because Kate and I want to have you to ourselves for a little while," Trace inserted smoothly, displaying a newfound sensitivity to Kathy's need of a sense of self-worth. "In time, we pray there will a brother or sister for you, baby," he continued, using Kate's endearment for the child. "But, until then, we have one another—don't we?"

The conversation of that evening replayed itself in Kate's mind at odd moments as the weeks until Christmas dwindled to days. During these odd moments, Kate couldn't avoid making a comparison between this holiday season and proceding ones, especially the last one.

The year before, Kate was feeling empty and very much alone and actually dreading the hype and hyperbole attached to the holiday. While Trace had been bitingly bitter and insensitive to his child's excitement and outspoken in his disgust of the whole thing.

The natural reaction to these moments of introspection was fear; so very happy and content was the Kate of his holiday season, she feared it could not possibly last.

And Kate was very happy and content. Her emotional fulfillment had begun when Trace had drawn her into his arms and whispered, "Come to me, my love."

With those five words, Trace had given her the hearth and home Kate had sought and feared would never be hers. The union of their bodies had always been satisfying physically. In the three months since Trace had made her his wife in a quiet, private ceremony with Kathy by his side, Kate had discovered a richly satisfying union of their minds.

The perfection of their wedding trip had less to do with the lush beauty of the island of Maui, and everything to do with the attitude of her husband.

Kate and Trace had married exactly one week after he'd come to her, heart in hand. During that hilariously frantic week they had cleaned out her apartment, sending the things she wanted to keep to San Antonio, and the stuff she didn't want to a local used furniture auctioneer. Kate gave a week's notice at work. She had also introduced Trace to her family with one breath and informed them of her plans to leave almost at once with him for Texas in the following breath.

Less than two hours after the ceremony uniting them, Kate, Trace and Kathy were on a plane bound eventually for Hawaii and a meeting with Trace's parents.

The elder Sinclairs had accepted Kate on sight. Trace and Kate had spent one day with his parents then, leaving Kathy in their capable care, they'd island-hopped to Maui to spend a few days alone.

Over three months later, Kate still thrilled to the mem
ory of the absolute bliss she'd experienced throughout the
entire length of their stay in Maui.

Kate had not expected the honeymoon conditions to
prevail once she and Trace had settled into his home out
side San Antonio. What she had steeled herself for was a
rather bumpy trial period while the three of them ad
justed to living together as a family.

On their return to Texas, Kate was pleasantly sur
prised to discover that no trial period of adjustment was
necessary. Kate readily admitted that it was Trace's atti
tude that was the cementing factor: when Trace Sinclair
decided to give of himself, he did so unconditionally.

Kate had slipped into the role of wife and mother as if
born to it—as, of course, she'd always known she was.
And, if she adored her new daughter, which she did, she
practically worshipped her husband. Both by word and
action, Trace reciprocated the commitment of self.

For Kate, emotional poverty had been exchanged for
emotional wealth. Kate shared her wealth generously.
There was laughter in the house outside San Antonio,
Texas.

As the clock ticked off the final minutes of Christmas
Eve, Kate sat on the floor near the sweetly aromatic,
brightly decorated balsam. The house, alive with the
joyous sound of happy inhabitants two hours before, was
now quiet except for the muted music of the season
wafting gently from the stereo in the corner of the living
room.

Trace had carried Kathy to bed hours before. Trace's
parents, visiting for the holidays, had remained to help

Trace and Kate "play" Santa Claus and have a light snack and a final drink before they too retired for the night.

Trace was in the kitchen loading the glasses and snacks plates into the dishwasher. Sitting amid the neatly arranged presents, Kate was once again lost in a reverie of comparison.

So much had happened in the space of one year; so many changes had occurred in that relatively short span. To Kate, it seemed much longer than one year since she'd endured the disillusionment of her parents' annual Christmas Eve circus. And even longer since she'd agreed to Trace's terms of a relationship and allowed him to undress her—quite like someone unwrapping an unexpected Christmas gift!

A soft smile curved Kate's lips at her unintentional analogy. But how very apt, she mused. She had given herself to Trace without qualm on Christmas Day, and in doing so had offered him her most precious gift...herself. Though Trace had made full use of her gift, Kate now knew that his total acceptance had come with the offering of himself in exchange.

"What are you thinking about?" Trace probed gently, settling next to her on the carpet while balancing a glass of wine in each hand.

"You and me and the Christmas tree," Kate murmured, her gaze pensive. Accepting the glass of wine, she tilted it to acknowledge his silent toast before continuing, "And the difference between this Christmas and last year."

"You mean, the difference in me," Trace smiled. "Don't you?"

"Yes." Kate smiled back. "You've been wonderful, Trace. I know how you feel about the holiday, yet you've gone out of your way to make it perfect for Kathy and me. You've been so thoughtful, so considerate through all the hectic activity and I wanted to—" Trace silenced her very effectively with a hard kiss.

"You know how I *used* to feel," Trace corrected her softly when he released her mouth. "I was miserable, honey. Miserable and bitter, and not too bright. I had always loved the holidays before my first marriage." He sighed deeply. "When the marriage ended I closed myself off to everything, every involvement, and cheated my daughter as well as myself."

Setting her glass aside, Kate cradled his face in her hands and drew his mouth to hers. "Oh, Trace, I love you so much!" she murmured passionately, kissing him fiercely.

Placing his glass next to hers, Trace slowly undressed her with trembling fingers. The tremor was mirrored in Kate's hands as she fumbled with his clothing. Then, the glow from the tree lights shimmering on their naked bodies, their whispered endearments blending with the joyful music, they exchanged the ultimate love gift of giving and receiving.

As the clock on the mantlepiece struck the hour of midnight, Kate and Trace lay entwined in a lovers' embrace beneath a tree resplendent with ornaments and lights, their breathing slowly returning to normal.

"I haven't been at all wonderful, Kate," Trace confessed, brushing his lips over her cheeks. "I needed this holiday desperately. I needed the love and laughter you've brought to my life, and my daughter, and this house."

Drawing Kate closer to his muscular strength, Trace caressed her with gentle hands and gazed down at her with eyes filled with a hint of wonder and a mist of tears.

"Happy birthday, honey." His lips took hers in a warm kiss. "Merry Christmas, darling." Again Trace bestowed the gift of his mouth. "I love you, my Kate."

Take 4
Silhouette Special Edition novels
FREE...

and preview future books in your home for 15 days!

Start with 4 FREE books, yours to keep. Then, preview 6 brand-new Special Edition® novels—delivered right to your door every month—as soon as they are published.

When you decide to keep them, pay just $1.95 each ($2.50 each in Canada), *with no shipping, handling, or other additional charges of any kind!*

Romance *is* alive, well and flourishing in the moving love stories presented by Silhouette Special Edition. They'll awaken your desires, enliven your senses, and leave you tingling all over with excitement. In each romance-filled story you'll live and breathe the emotions of love and the satisfaction of romance triumphant.

You won't want to miss a single one of the heart-felt stories presented by Silhouette Special Edition; and when you take advantage of this special offer, you won't have to.

You'll also receive a FREE subscription to the Silhouette Books Newsletter as long as you remain a member. Each lively issue is filled with news on upcoming titles, interviews with your favorite authors, even their favorite recipes.

To become a home subscriber and receive your first 4 books FREE, fill out and mail the coupon today!

Silhouette Special Edition®

Silhouette Books, 120 Brighton Rd., P.O. Box 5084, Clifton, NJ 07015-5084

Clip and mail to: Silhouette Books, 120 Brighton Road, P.O. Box 5084, Clifton, NJ 07015-5084*

YES. Please send me 4 FREE Silhouette Special Edition novels. Unless you hear from me after I receive them, send me 6 new Silhouette Special Edition novels to preview each month. I understand you will bill me just $1.95 each, a total of $11.70 (in Canada, $2.50 each, a total of $15.00), with no shipping, handling, or other charges of any kind. There is no minimum number of books that I must buy, and I can cancel at any time. The first 4 books are mine to keep.   **BS28R6**

Name _____ (please print)

Address _____ Apt. #

City _____ State/Prov. _____ Zip/Postal Code

* In Canada, mail to: Silhouette Canadian Book Club, 320 Steelcase Rd., E., Markham, Ontario, L3R 2M1, Canada

Terms and prices subject to change.

SILHOUETTE SPECIAL EDITION is a service mark and registered trademark.   SE-SUB-2

Take 4
Silhouette Intimate Moments novels
FREE...

If you're the kind of woman who wants more passion from your romance novels...

... preview 4 brand new Silhouette Intimate Moments® novels—delivered right to your door every month—for 15 days as soon as they are published. When you decide to keep them, you pay just $2.25 each ($2.50 each, in Canada), *with no shipping, handling, or other charges of any kind!*

These romance novels are not for everyone. They were created to give you a more detailed, more exciting reading experience, filled with romantic fantasy...dynamic, contemporary characters... involving stories...intense sensuality and stirring passion.

Silhouette Desire

COMING NEXT MONTH

CAUTIOUS LOVER—Stephanie James
Jess Winter was a cautious lover, but Elly Trent knew there was warmth locked beneath his controlled facade. Perhaps playing the seductress would provide the key. . . .

WHEN SNOW MEETS FIRE—Christine Flynn
Life in the frozen beauty of the Aleutian islands was exactly what Dr. Tory Richards needed, until things started to heat up when steel-eyed Nick Spencer literally crashed into her world.

HEAVEN ON EARTH—Sandra Kleinschmit
When Samantha met Jason she felt as if she had stepped into a romance novel. But when she learned that he was actually her favorite romance author, fact became stranger than fiction.

NO MAN'S KISSES—Nora Powers
Hilary had always tried to avoid Justin Porter, but now a debt forced her to work on his ranch. Could she prevent herself from falling under his spell again?

THE SHADOW BETWEEN—Diana Stuart
The sale of the McLeod mansion drew Alida Drury and Justin McLeod together in the game of intrigue and romance that strangely echoed the past and cast shadows on the future.

NOTHING VENTURED—Suzanne Simms
Wisconsin librarian Mary Beth Williams took a gamble and headed for Las Vegas in search of excitement. She found it when she met Nick Durand and hit the jackpot of romance.

AVAILABLE NOW:

A MUCH NEEDED HOLIDAY
Joan Hohl

MOONLIGHT SERENADE
Laurel Evans

HERO AT LARGE
Aimée Martel

TEACHER'S PET
Ariel Berk

HOOK, LINE AND SINKER
Elaine Camp

LOVE BY PROXY
Diana Palmer